HUMOUR 12⁹⁵

D0033884

45 Acres of Fun & Tears

WITHDRAWN

SEP 0 2 2020

UNBC Library

Also by Jim Morrison:

Foxy Freddy And His Friends (with Al Morrison)
Foxy Freddy's Bicentennial Party
If You Want To . . . WRITE!

45 Acres
of Fun & Tears

Jim Morrison

Goose Lane Editions

©Jim Morrison, 1989
All rights reserved. No part of this work may be reproduced or used in any form or by any means, electronic or mechanical, including photocopying, recording, or any information storage and retrieval system, without the prior written permission of the publisher. Requests for photocopying of any part of this book shall be directed in writing to the Canadian Reprography Collective, 379 Adelaide Street West, Suite M1, Toronto, Ontario, Canada M5V 1S5.

Published with the assistance of the Canada Council, the New Brunswick Department of Tourism, Recreation and Heritage, and the University of New Brunswick, 1989.

Cover and interior illustrations by Angela Webb O'Hara
Book design by Julie Scriver
Printed in Canada by Wilson Printing

Canadian Cataloguing in Publication Data

Morrison, Jim.
45 acres of fun and tears

ISBN 0-86492-112-8

1. Morrison, Jim. 2. Farm life—New Brunswick—Humor.
I. Title. II. Title: Forty-five acres of fun and tears.

S522.C2M67 1989   630'.2'017 C89-098639-8

Goose Lane Editions Ltd.
248 Brunswick Street,
Fredericton, New Brunswick,
Canada E3B 1G9

This book is dedicated to Kay, who shared a dream and was the moving force that made it all come true. Everyone should be so lucky!

Contents

Foreword

That old adage, "You can take the boy out of the country but you can't take the country out of the boy," is not entirely true. Not in my case. During the Depression years, while Dad was trying to wrestle a living out of his music, announcing on radio and living in Saint John, Mother and three children lived in Avondale, Carleton County, at the small farm of my maternal grandfather, Samuel G. Barter. I knew and loved farm life, working with the one horse Sam owned, on occasion trying to milk his one cow, feeding chickens and pigs, moving hay around in the very dusty loft, pitching hay high onto a wagon, making rare trips to Hartland or Woodstock by way of horse and wagon or, in winter, by sleigh. Even walking a mile to the one-room, eight-grade school during fall, winter and spring was more of a challenge than a hardship.

In those days many students from rural one-room schools did not continue their education beyond Grade 8, if they remained that long. Attending High School, then Grades 9-11 inclusive, meant leaving the country and going to a town or city, paying board or living with relatives. Many rural families could not afford the cost.

Dad decided it was time to take the plunge, depression or no depression, and move the family to the Saint John area. We settled in Glen Falls, now part of the city, and sister Margery was the first of the family to attend Saint John High School.

The move to the port city did not end my country life; I still spent my summers at Avondale, right up to the time I joined the Royal Canadian Navy in 1940. I have never lost my love for the country; I have never enjoyed living in cities or towns. I've lived in some big ones, including Toronto, Halifax, Regina, Milford (Connecticut), Saint John, Fredericton, Dallas (Texas), and towns such as St. Stephen and Woodstock. During five years in the navy and forty as a journalist I never abandoned my dream of finding my own place in the country, some day, somewhere, a spot to call my own and finally sink my roots. It is a dream cherished by many men and women.

If I ever did have any skills working on the farm, they disappeared somewhere along the line. There have been some humorous experiences as this citified klutz tried to re-adapt to rural life, and there have been moments of pathos and poignancy.

I may have lost the skills and physical strength to farm effectively but I have never regretted my decision to return to rural life, to slow the pace, to enjoy the peace and tranquility of the country.

There's no stigma attached to being a klutz in any field. It can be funny at times, sad at others. What the experience has taught me is the truth that if you want something badly enough, work hard at accomplishing your dream, plan well and be ready to make the necessary sacrifices, then there's every chance that you will succeed. Sharing some of the adventures we have had at Twin Pines Farm is my way of saying, in the words of Bob Hope's theme song: "Thanks for the memories." Perhaps too it will encourage others to pursue their dreams. They can come true!

Jim Morrison
Wakefield, 1989

1
Searching for a Dream

The gravel driveway was rough, deep troughs eroded by rain runoff, as we drove cautiously up the steep, curving grade. Behind us, across the highway, the setting sun painted the St. John River in tints of red and gold. Had we finally found our dream retirement home, a farmhouse and a few acres of land? Northampton was only a few miles from Woodstock but did have what we were looking for: beautiful country living with spectacular scenery. The St. John River Valley, particularly in Carleton County, offers dramatic panoramas as you drive along either Route 103 or Route 105, on opposite sides of the river.

Those fortunate enough to have homes overlooking the valley and river in the Woodstock area have a choice: you can enjoy watching the sun rise if you have a house along Route 103 (the Woodstock side); you'll enjoy technicolor sunsets if you live along Route 105 (the Hartland side of the river).

The house we were going to inspect was off Route 105 on the east side of the river and as we stepped out of the car and looked west we were dazzled by the breathtaking sunset.

"Wow! Imagine watching this view every night," I said, bubbling with excitement. "The scene itself is worth the price of the place."

"Come back to earth, boy," Kay cautioned. "We haven't seen the house yet and we're not going to make up our minds on scenery alone. We've come too far for snap decisions."

She was right, of course. As usual. I'm the impulsive one in the family and she usually has to put up with the consequences of my habit of rushing into matters without looking ahead. Both New Brunswickers, we were back in the province for a visit while living in Connecticut. We had decided to locate a country place that would eventually be a good retirement home. We chose Carleton County as the ideal location, both because of strong family ties to the country and because we had lived in Woodstock and knew the town and its people.

As we turned from watching the red and gold sunset and studied the exterior of the weather-beaten old farmhouse, I had a sinking sensation in my stomach. It was, at best, what is described in real estate classified ads as a "handyman's dream." Ignoring the euphemism, in the more real world it needed a lot of hard work and an infusion of many dollars to make it presentable. So did the yard and surrounding fields. This baby hadn't had a caring mother for a long time. It would be a challenge to take a property being reclaimed by nature and groom it until it again became a country garden picture of shining white home, verdant lawns and groomed landscaping.

What may have been a lawn had been transformed by high grass and weeds; determined burdocks pushed their elephant ears skyward and stubborn Scotch thistles thrust their lavender flowers arrogantly among the nodding heads of timothy. Rusted pieces of abandoned junk were sharp reminders of better times in the past. Only the clean smell of the air, the night calls of birds and the spectacular sunset provided relief from the dismal scene.

As I inserted the old fashioned key in the old fashioned lock I had a feeling that the final decision had already been made. My worst fears were realized as I threw open the door and invited Kay to step in. The place was a shambles. A house unoccupied is no longer a home. It could be a real beauty, I thought, as I studied the floors, walls, ceilings, and carved woodwork. Even while outside I had noticed the remarkable sturdiness of the old house, built before the throwaway era. This wasn't two-by-four framing. There was evidence of huge hand-hewn beams and solid struts. The frame seemed rock solid.

"Look at those wide pine boards in the floor," I said to Kay, my enthusiasm again bubbling. "You can't get lumber like that anymore. Boy, that could be refinished and come up looking like new."

"Sure," Kay said in a tone just short of sarcasm, pointing at the stained wallpaper peeling from the walls, "and that could look like new too after a lot of hard work."

"It sure could," I replied, "look at that!" I pulled on a piece of torn wallpaper, the better to show her the wide boards that had been split to hold the lime plaster. This was an historic building, erected with loving care to last and last. "You don't find this kind of a house anymore," I said. "We can restore it and have a home that's as solid as the day this one was built."

Kay sighed mightily. "What's with this 'we' stuff? We both know who'll have to do the work. A country carpenter you're not!"

True. Neither am I a plumber, electrician, cabinet maker, painter, wallpaper hanger, cattleman, architect, engineer or farmer. Still, I had ambitions to dabble in all of these and this would be a perfect place to do it. It soon became apparent, as we examined the rooms of this venerable house, that I'd have to be a Jack-of-all-trades to restore this once fine building to its original glory. It could be done, if you had unlimited money to hire the professional tradespeople necessary. That we didn't (and don't) have!

"Here's the water supply," I said, as we entered a back room, once the kitchen, and saw a black plastic pipe dribbling water into a stained white sink. I leaned over and slurped a mouthful. "That's really cold, and good tasting."

Kay looked even more distressed than she had when we entered the house. "That's it, Jim, no way!" she said in a tone that wouldn't be challenged.

"But that's spring water from up the hill," I protested. "It wouldn't be much of a job to have it piped in properly, put in a pressure pump, plumbing, new sinks, and a renovated bathroom with tub and shower. That's wonderful water!"

"And I'm not going to become a pioneer at this stage of my life," Kay said emphatically. "This is a great old house and it offers a wonderful opportunity for restoration, for someone to turn it into their 'dream home.' The view is tremendous and there's a possibility to raise animals and poultry and to do some small farming. And, it's not for us!"

We left the house, locked the front door, and climbed into the car. I was still muttering about a lost opportunity, a clear picture of that completely restored house and property vivid in my mind.

"If we hurry we can still visit that riverside place in Wakefield," Kay said quietly. "Maybe that will be our 'dream' come true."

I smiled. I love adventure and there was another one just ahead.

2
Land But No House!

The sun had hidden below the western horizon as Kay and I stood in a field just off Route 103 in Wakefield, golden-red clouds above the high hill on the eastern side of the St. John River reflecting the dying rays of old Sol. It was quiet, peaceful, a light breeze composing background music for both grasses and weeds as they performed a slow twilight dance. Blackbirds swooped above a canopy of alders and the lonesome cry of a loon rose clearly in the evening air.

"Do you feel it?" I asked Kay. "This is magic."

"Maybe we have found the place for our dream home," she replied.

Her choice of words was on the money. Certainly there was no house in our immediate view on this property, dream or otherwise. No house, no barn, no machine shed, no outbuildings. Not even an outhouse. This was an old farm established in the 1880s, an original land grant.

A large map of Carleton County, New Brunswick, published in 1876 is one of our proudest possessions. It names the owners of every piece of property in the county. The farm land on which we were standing was then owned by D. Dickensen, according to the map, and was later known as the Saunders farm. It stretched from the St. John River uphill and back, for 185 acres more or less. The farm had changed hands a number of times during the hundred plus years since it had been sculptured out of the forest. No buildings remained to tell the history of its previous owners. Fire had wiped out most of the significant traces of the previous occupants. We were to discover that not all traces had been eliminated.

"Well, we can't see much more tonight and it's getting darker by the minute," I said. "I can hardly wait to come back tomorrow."

"Me too," she replied. "I want to get down to the river and see what's there. Perhaps we'll be able to spot that loon family. I have a good feeling about this place; it's something that's hard to put into words."

She didn't have to. I had the same reaction, a sense of belonging, of having found a rare jewel. It was almost mystical, a new experience. Pure romanticism, I thought, struggling to return to my natural pragmatism.

What had happened was the culmination of a series of happenings and moods: an unusually beautiful sunset, a desire to find the "right" place, a view that was almost overwhelming, and our anxiety to make a land decision before our return to Connecticut. My heart told me that my pragmatic self had lost this time. As if to emphasize the point, the spine-tingling cry of a loon pierced the still night, a call that seemed to be urging us to "come back soon."

Kay was quiet as we drove back to Woodstock where we were staying with daughter Beth and her husband, Robert (Bob) MacFarlane, in an old 13-room house we had owned before moving to Connecticut. I refrained from breaking the spell, respecting her silence, allowing her the space she needed. It's going to be an interesting day tomorrow, I thought; so much to see and do.

As usual, Kay and I were up with the sun. We always are. We're early to bed, early to rise people. We had our breakfasts, then climbed into our car for the seven mile drive to Wakefield.

As we swung off the highway onto the tracks of what used to be a driveway, now heavily grassed, the sun was already over the top of the hill across the St. John River. Now we could see the startling green of the valley on both sides. A few old farmhouses nestled on the slope on the east side, some meadows running almost to the river below Route 105, others reaching toward the summit of the hill.

Mixed stands of evergreen, alders, poplars and hardwoods, combined with fields of hay, grain, pasture and potatoes created a crazy quilt of various shades of green. From our vantage point near Route 103 we could see little of what this farm property might promise. There were potato fields on either side of the grass-covered driveway so the farm wasn't entirely fallow.

"They must be leasing some of the land to a farmer around here," I suggested. "It's good there are crops in, land needs to be worked." "We can't see too much from here," Kay said. "There seems to be a ridge that hides much of the land between here and the river. Let's walk down the driveway a bit."

She was right. There was a ridge that hid from view the lower part of the property and soon we came to the ruins of the old farmhouse, now nothing but a rubble-filled hole in the ground with pieces of rusted iron from beds and stoves, an old hot water heater, a blackened and rusty washing machine and the charred remains of furniture.

Though the contents of the house that survived the fire had fallen into the basement, the flat rock cellar walls still stood upright, sentinels guarding the ruins of the old home. We could see that the house had been positioned in a strategic spot, one that gave a nerve-pulsing view of the river and the valley hill beyond.

The ground sloped steeply from the old foundation and about fifty feet below, a cow path had been branded into the side hill by the passing of thousands of split hooves over many years.

"This is the perfect place for our house when we build," Kay said, her blue eyes sweeping left and right, taking in an old apple tree just thirty feet away and another larger one to the right near the cow path.

"Whoa there, girl," I cautioned. "We have to see a lot more before we make any decisions and we still don't know the price, or if we can afford this property." Despite my words, I knew she was right. This is what we had been searching for.

It didn't look it to the naked eye. I frowned as I looked over the potato fields between the foundation and the road. The furrows were parallel to the driveway, running up and down hill. This was (and is) a "no-no" for most farmers, an invitation to costly erosion. The hill sloped even more steeply from the foundation to the river. Alders had taken over a good part of what had been pasture. A wide band of trees stretched into the sky between the lower alders and the river.

We strolled over the fields and discovered there had been barn on both sides of the old foundation. One was close to the house ruins, just cement and rocks where once had been a sturdy barn or an outbuilding of some kind. Because of its nearness to the house we speculated that it may have been a combination building to stable horses and cows, and probably a hen-house.

A bit uphill from the ruins of the farm we found a well, fifteen feet deep, with a circular wall of flat field stones, some of which had collapsed into the water. We learned later that this well had provided the water for the house and the livestock.

The second barn, located about 300 feet from the house, had been a huge one before fire reduced it to rubble. A solid cement foundation remained. I paced it off and estimated that the building must have been ninety feet long and about thirty wide, or close to it. It probably had a high peak with a capacity to hold many hundreds of tons of loose hay.

"This has great potential for some kind of an outbuilding," I said. "The cement is still in good condition and has a solid base on which to erect some kind of a building."

Kay laughed. "And why would we need a ninety foot barn? We'll be lucky if we can afford to build a house, let alone barns and sheds." Her smile belied the sting of her words.

I shook my head and grinned, scuffling at the rough texture of the top of the cement wall. We both knew that someday, somehow, I'd probably try to build something on the old foundation, even if I didn't know how to erect an outhouse.

"Hey, there's a break in the alders," Kay said, pointing, "and look at those berries. Let's walk down to the river."

The berries were deep purple chokecherries, tart to the tongue but the basic ingredient for a spectacular homemade wine. Cherry trees were found all the way to the river, following a rock pile downhill. This untidy pile of stones of all shapes and sizes was mute testimony to the thousands of hours previous occupants of the farm had spent in clearing the stony Carleton County land. There were other reminders: apples trees gone wild, crabapple trees, a few clearings in the woods, indications of former rough roads and trails. We soon passed through the alders that had claimed a former pasture and entered a mixed forest of evergreens, maples, white birch, beechnut, butternut, basswood, black cherry, oak and several other species I couldn't identify. Hazelnut bushes were spotted here and there and large, tough, wild grapevines snaked their way up through the branches of trees. What a wonderful opportunity for nature walks, I thought, if we can only carve out some trails.

The hill had been steep as we stumbled our way down through bushes and raspberry canes fighting to claim the old path but it levelled off as we neared the river. Suddenly there was a circular clearing ahead, dominated by two towering butternut trees at either side.

"Oh, look at the ostrich ferns!" Kay cried, running to one edge of the clearing where she picked a long, delicate frond. "That means we'll have our own fiddleheads."

A gully ran alongside the upriver edge of the clearing and it did indeed have a large patch of ostrich ferns, now several feet high and nodding gently in the light breeze. Looking to the other side of the clearing I could see an even deeper gully, surely a stream bed during spring runoff, and it too was populated with the popular ostrich fern.

We walked across the small open meadow, wondering why it was there, and followed a much worn path to the river, past a huge old maple that was partly dead with much of the main trunk hollow (an obvious home for wild bees, upper hollow branches being used by birds and squirrels for homes). We found another large clearing on the river bank. Large patches of ostrich fern swayed in the breeze both up and down river.

On that particular day the mighty St. John River didn't look or smell like the river I had once fished, prior to construction of the Mactaquac dam. It had been fast-moving water then, with large islands and famous salmon pools. Now it was stagnant, still, polluted with effluent from sources upriver where raw sewage emptied into it at numerous points.

"I sure wouldn't want to go swimming in there," I said to Kay, wrinkling my nose in disgust. "Nor would any self respecting fish."

We saw no loon family on that first visit, neither did we see any ducks. A couple of seagulls, 150 miles from their home port of Saint John at the mouth of the river, bobbed in the sluggish brown water about midstream.

We didn't take time to explore the complete waterfront of the property. We had been told the farm had a quarter of a mile frontage on the river. We did, however, do a bit more exploring around the river bank clearing and found another less than fifty feet downriver, one crowded with a hugh pile of logs and heavy long planks. We were puzzled by a twelve foot length of chain with mammoth links, each twelve inches or more in length, and wondered about its use. Oh well, I thought, there's a lot to learn about this place and I'll just add the massive chain to the growing list of mysteries to be solved.

We were now hot, tired and thirsty and started back for the car. We hadn't realized just how steep the hill was until we struggled back up, taking frequent stops to draw on reserve energy. We were puffing and drenched with sweat by the time we arrived at the cement foundation of the old barn and had another rest before strolling to our vehicle.

"Well, what do you think, Kay?" I asked, certain in my own mind that this was the answer we both had in mind as the place to put down our roots. That was important to us. There had been little permanence in our life thus far; after five years in the Navy during the Second World War, it seemed that I had struggled constantly for new experiences and to develop my writing skills. There had been many moves, a string of homes and apartments, from Saint John to Toronto, from Fredericton to Woodstock to Connecticut, including return trips to several of those cities.

Kay wore an impish smile as she looked around, absorbing the eye-pleasing sight of the riverside forest, the crowded alders, pasture land being reclaimed by nature, tall grasses and colorful weeds, and the spectacular panoramic view of the river and the hill opposite reaching to billowy white clouds in a blue sky. "It just might do," she said, smiling with obvious relish. "Yes, sir, this may just be the place."

A familiar sound from the river broke into our thoughts, like a freight train clattering along steel rails, but how could that be? I looked more closely at the opposite shore and thought I could see light reflecting from metal. Perhaps there was a train track there. The noise intensified as we looked up and down river. Then, from the south, a black diesel engine appeared hauling a dozen boxcars, flatbeds and a caboose. The track ran parallel to the river on the east side of the valley, apparently only twenty feet or so above the water.

"It looks like the Toonerville Trolley," I said, referring to a famous comic strip of many years ago. "That really adds to the scenery."

"It's like a postcard," Kay said softly. "I wish I'd brought my camera along."

"I think we'll have many chances to get that picture," I said. "Let's go and figure out what we're going to do — and when."

We took a final look towards the ruins of the old farmhouse. Two lonely pines thrust into the sky, their limbs tightly ensnarled, wide trunks only four feet apart forming a natural gate. They were only forty feet from the fieldstone walls of the house foundation.

"That would be a great name for our place," I said. "Twin Pines Farm."

3

Chasing a Dream

A dream unnurtured is a dream abandoned. People often dream of a new car, a boat, a home, a new job, a career change, a place in the country or a condo in the city, and do nothing to achieve the dream except, perhaps, to buy more lottery tickets. Those who make dreams come true have to take a long range view, blueprint their goals, take the necessary steps to separate reality from fantasy. There's usually no quick fix. You work and you sacrifice and you win. Locating a piece of land we wanted was comparatively easy, an adventure in itself. Now it was time for the long range planning, drawing a blueprint that would guide us step by step through the years until our retirement home became a reality at Twin Pines Farm. First, how big a piece of land could we afford? We didn't need an 185 acre farm, nor could we raise the money, in all probability. Would the seller be willing to subdivide the property, possibly only that portion between the highway and the river? We were determined that we wanted frontage on the water. We also sought a piece of land where we could build a house and not be crowded by neighbors, no matter how cooperative and friendly. We had lived in towns and cities far too long. We wanted some space.

When we returned to Connecticut we still hadn't purchased the property. We had been assured we could buy the piece of land between the highway and the river, a block of about forty-five acres with a quarter of a mile frontage on the highway and on the water. The price had been determined, a bargain at 1989 land values in Carleton County and a good deal in the 1960s. Still, it was a lot of money for us, particularly as we had a lovely home in Milford, Connecticut, and carried a heavy mortgage. Negotiations continued by mail and an agreement was finally reached. We signed the papers and took on another mortgage during our next visit to Carleton County.

It was to be several more years before we were ready to leave and return to New Brunswick, a decision that did not come easily because we had become very attached to Connecticut, our work there, and the new friends we had made. Selling the house in Milford was not easy because the country was in the middle of a recession. We had purchased in boom times and were selling during a bust. Nor was it easy to sell our second car, a Corvair convertible we had come to love (Ralph Nader to the contrary), but a number of trips to New Brunswick had convinced us that the Corvair must go, that we could get neither parts nor service if we took it along. So they went: house and car. You don't sell at a profit during a bust. Time to tighten the belt.

Once again I was back at *The Telegraph-Journal* and *The Evening Times-Globe* in Saint John, where I had first started my newspaper career after leaving the Navy in 1945. Our new home, briefly, was a handsome old house in East Riverside, with a spectacular panoramic view of the Kennebecasis River, particularly at sunset. We were within walking distance of the championship Riverside golf club. Unfortunately, I didn't hang around long enough to take up the game. I was offered the challenge of a new position in Fredericton at *The Daily Gleaner*, another newspaper on which I had apprenticed on a number of desks. It was a challenge I accepted. We were in Elm City before the dust had hardly settled on our luggage. One factor that tilted the scales in favor of the move was that it would bring us that much closer to Twin Pines Farm. That would mean more frequent visits to our "country estate," most weekends and as many other days as could be squeezed in.

Even during those last years in Connecticut we had paid numerous visits to the Wakefield property, taking great pleasure in walking the woods, planning for future gardens, perhaps a pond, certainly a sanctuary for wildlife, the carving of trails through the woods, the preservation of the numerous wildflowers — trillium, blue, yellow and white violets, Jacks-in-the-pulpit — so they would continue to grace the land with their presence.

We found that wild strawberries grew in abundance in the old pastures, as did wild raspberries. The latter continued to spread over the land uncontrolled, seasonal home to many families of red-winged blackbirds. The apples and crabapples were nothing to brag about though it was obvious the old farm had once supported a fair sized orchard. Years of neglect took their toll, as did diseases and insects; the fruit from these trees was misshapen, scabby and wormy. We decided to keep the trees because they offered support and shelter for the birds. We're birdwatchers and we want to have as many around as we can attract.

The old budget was strained once again after the move to Fredericton and the purchase of yet another new home and yet another mortgage. Visits to Twin Pines Farm became more frequent and more enjoyable, as we were now only an hour and a half away, portal to portal. Our blueprint for the future was still intact and we were more or less on schedule. There was more demand on my time and energy with the change of position, adding to my enjoyment of a trip to the farm. The only way we could spend the night at the farm was to pitch a tent or take a trailer-camper. Neither alternative appealed to us. We had paid our dues in leaking tents and primitive camping while the children were growing up. Enough's enough. Kay and I were both country folk, in spirit and in upbringing, but we were not campers. We looked for another solution to the problem of a temporary shelter at the farm.

The solution presented itself in an advertisement in the local newspaper, a Fredericton area company trumpeting the merits of their prefab cottages and camps. We visited a model camp, were impressed, and decided to have one erected at the farm. Once located on the site of the old farmhouse, the camp appeared to be nothing more than a large rectangular box. It had a good roof, strong plywood siding, windows and doors, and not much else. It certainly lacked glamor. It was even more simple inside, two-by-four partitions with cheap paneling closing off a couple of bedrooms and a tiny bathroom. The remainder of the interior was a kitchen and living space. There were no interior doors, not even for the small bathroom. Curtains and drapes were used for privacy; they were able to keep eyes from prying but did nothing to mute sounds. This was as primitive as we were willing to get. The bathroom had no bath, no sink, no running water and no toilet. The purchase of a portable chemical outfit saved many trips to the alders for relief. It also accounted for many trips to the outdoors as the honey pot had to be emptied at least once a day, meaning that holes had to be dug and filled in. There was no electricity. Propane gas provided fuel for the kitchen range and for special lighting. Still, this arrangement was a vast improvement over a tent or a camper-trailer as far as we were concerned and we could also accommodate overnight guests.

Water was carried from a spring excavated on the side hill near the cottage. The deep well that had served previous occupants of this farm for so many years could not be used. The fieldstones from the top, down about five feet, had given up the fight, and collapsed into the well below. It would be a tremendous job to get the large stones out, to rehabilitate the well. We built a plank platform and covered it over to prevent tragedy and relied on the spring for our cooking and drinking water.

It may have been primitive living but we've never had happier times than those at the Twin Pines Farm cottage. We had both been brought up in homes that had no electricity, no central heating. We were familiar with trips to the old outdoor two-seater outhouse. Carrying water for use was not a new experience. The propane gas mantles gave much better light than the kerosene lamps of our childhood days. The chemical toilet was an improvement over the two-seater, and emptying the honey pot was no different than dumping the thunder jugs of earlier days. What really mattered was that we had a roof over our heads at Twin Pines Farm. The camp-cottage wasn't on our original blueprint of plans for the future but it proved to be an excellent move. Now we could arrive at the farm and stay for the entire weekend, without bothering other people to put us up for a night or two or more.

More time at the farm meant getting into more mischief, of course. First I decided the alders must go, they were taking over the farm below the ridge. My blueprint for the future didn't indicate in any way what I might want to use the land for once the alders had been removed. No sir, they just had to go. They were encroaching on land that had once been good pasture. The alders had their own secret. Once those nearest the cottage had been cut down we discovered they had been hiding the body of an old car. It was the first indication we had that the alders were all that kept secret the fact that Twin Pines Farm was a junkyard. There were other cars and parts of cars, abandoned washing machines, hot water boilers, pieces of machinery, even an old rusty hay rake. The alders, we decided, would continue in their role as hiders of junk — as soon as they could grow back again. They have flourished with renewed energy and now claim several more acres than they did when so brutally attacked with axe and chain saw.

The red-winged blackbirds have never thanked us, formally. They should be grateful. The first year we were at the cottage in late summer we discovered that Twin Pines Farm is the site for the gathering of the clans for blackbirds. Our resident blackbirds, now accompanied by their summer-born offspring, must learn to share their territory with their loud cousins. They come by the thousands, dark clouds of them swooping in each night to roost in the alders and whooshing away in spiral clouds in the morning to feed in nearby fields.

Each year the farm is host to a number of blackbird families, each male staking his own territory and proudly displaying his red flashes as he tries to attract a mate, and warn off other males. They raise their families, first nesting in patches of wild raspberry canes, then hiding in the alders. The grand exodus, the start of the annual migration south, comes in late summer. Then the Twin Pines Farm blackbirds are joined by their grandfathers and grandmothers, mothers and fathers, uncles and aunts, cousins by the hundreds, plus a few grackles and starlings who don't realize they're not blackbirds.

So the alders won their right to stay for a number of reasons. The wild raspberry canes stayed too, even though they may eventually take over the farm if they're not stopped. These particular raspberry canes are not useful for their berries. They are almost barren, more interested in proliferating than in producing fruit. They serve a twofold purpose: they make wonderful and safe nesting sanctuaries for birds; their strong root systems play an important role in holding the thin earth that covers this river-valley gravel pit.

Five years after getting the camp-cottage we had become very attached to the farm and decided that the next phase of our blueprint should be adopted soon. We had learned a lot during that time, including the fact that it did indeed have good stands of fiddleheads in the spring, though much depended on the ferocity of the spring freshet.

We were told that the huge pile of logs and heavy planks was a reminder of river drives of the past when loggers herded their winter's cut down the St. John River to mills. The formidable chain with its foot-long links was used to anchor the holding boom of logs and planks to the opposite shore to another anchorage. Old roads and trails through the woods marked where the river men had brought in supplies.

We were frustrated when we discovered that tons of the farm's riverbank disappeared each year during the spring runoff, thanks to the Mactaquac dam erected by the New Brunswick Electric Power Commission. Slabs of ice tear at the banks as the raging river churns by. When we first arrived at the farm and visited the river, orange ribbons tied ten feet up the trunks of trees and as far back as fifteen feet from the water, marked the land claimed by NB Power. In other words, river land property owners had lost for all time their river frontage. Since that first visit and successive spring floods the freshets have carved into the bank ever more deeply. Even the beribboned trees have been torn from the earth by the combination of angry freshet and huge blocks of ice and swept downriver.

Yet the annual spring freshet, regardless of its ferocity, is just one of the spectacular sights to be seen at Twin Pines Farm throughout the year, morning, evening and all day.

4
Bees Are Buzzing!

The morning sun had kissed the earth and the dew had dried on the meadow grass as Robert MacFarlane and I strolled along the old cow path at the farm, a familiar habit since the cottage had been erected. Dandelion suns danced in the stunted green grass as waves of heat rose from the meadow, accentuating the fresh, earthy smell of spring. We were checking the possibility of establishing a Christmas tree plantation to make better use of some of the treeless vacant land.

We were quite a distance from the cottage when I got an urgent call from nature, with no time to sprint back to the chemical toilet. It was an emergency and I scrabbled frantically behind a ten foot spruce and dropped my jeans. Everything was routine until I pulled up my blue shorts.

"There's a bee in my shorts!" I roared in shock, leaping to my feet, my jeans falling around my ankles. An angry buzzing came from inside my shorts and I feared for the worst. I quickly crouched and pulled down my underwear and a bumblebee zoomed off with its afterburners on full thrust, obviously as startled as I was, or more so.

Robert rolled on the ground, laughing so hard it brought tears to his eyes. "That was the funniest sight I've ever seen," he gasped, cackling like a hen that had laid a double yoke egg. "You should have seen your face, and you broke all records for a high jump."

It wasn't funny for me, at the time. My adrenal glands had pushed into the red danger-zone and my heart pounded furiously. Recreating what had happened, it seemed that a bee had been minding its own business, gathering nectar from one of the large dandelions when I had my emergency. He was caught in my shorts when I pulled them up, and he was brushed off the flower and trapped. Evidently the bee was too scared to sting because I escaped from the adventure with nothing worse than a near heart attack.

I have a phobia about insects, one that has remained with me as long as I can remember. I'm scared of all creepy-crawlies and flying bugs and flies, whether they be mosquitoes, blackflies, no-see-ums, dragon flies, spiders and, particularly, bees, hornets and wasps.

My fears started early in life while I was living at Grandfather Sam Barter's home in Avondale, a small farm that boasted many types of creepy-crawlies and flying, stinging insects. He kept a single hive of honey bees and I can still see him working around that white box, bare arms and no hat and veil for protection.

On certain days, however — and he seemed to have an instinct that warned him — he would put on protective clothing while working around the hive. He would coax me to come and help, assuring me there was nothing to fear. I had nothing to fear but fear itself. That was enough and still is. Somewhere, sometime I must have been stung and the experience terrified me. I can't remember when or where: the circumstances are deeply buried in my psyche, but the fear remains to this day.

It was to be reinforced by several incidents at Twin Pines Farm long after the adventure of trapping a bumblebee in my shorts. There was the occasion, for instance, when son-in-law Robert decided he'd like to have a hive of honey bees. I didn't object to his dream, neither did I encourage it. Robert pushed on with his project, attending meetings of beekeepers, seeking knowledge on the raising of bees and purchasing the necessary equipment.

He finally gathered together the necessary components for a hive, and obtained the necessary tools and machinery to extract the honey when the proper time arrived. His first year was at least a partial success, and he was able to obtain quite a few pounds of honey. The second season seemed to be going well, and Robert was faced with the problem of his hive swarming, a not uncommon occurrence when a colony grows beyond the limits of space available. Beekeepers try to retrieve the swarm and have a second hive ready for occupancy. Robert's hive was located in a meadow north of the cottage, several hundred meters away. When part of the colony swarmed they became a milling mass on a tree not far from their original home and were comparatively easy to capture.

The honey bee is of the genus *Apis mellifera* (or *mellifica*) with most of those raised in New Brunswick of the Italian variety. Each colony has a queen, thousands of workers (sexually undeveloped females) and a few hundred drones (fertile males). During a nuptial flight the queen is pursued by the drones. The unlucky male that mates with the queen impregnates her with millions of sperm — and then he dies. When a hive swarms, a new queen, drawn from the ranks of workers, is created as the mother of a new colony. The Italian variety of honey bee is not a killer bee so-called. But any stinging bee can cause death to a human.

Robert's experiment with raising honey bees came to a terrifying and almost tragic end one hot August day. Kay and I and Beth were in the cottage, I having declined for the millionth time Robert's invitation to accompany him while he attended his hives. There was nothing unusual about the day but something most unusual was taking place at the hive. Our fearless beekeeper was attacked!

The first we knew of the incident was when we heard Robert screaming for help, his cries more piercing as he came closer to the cottage. There was also a spine-chilling and ominous drone or buzzing, a terrifying sound similar to that used for special effects in a disaster movie. Suddenly Robert ran into our view, his arms flailing, his red face contorted through the dark veil of his beekeeper's hat. He was surrounded by thousands of angry, aggressive honey bees, all trying to find a way to penetrate his protective clothing and sting their opponent. It was a sight we'll never forget, one that froze the mind in horror. Though he wore coveralls that protected him from neck to feet and a hat and veil that should have guarded his head, face and neck, it was obvious that Robert had been stung and was hurting, to say nothing of the state of his mind as he vainly tried to fight off the army of enraged bees. We were overcome with dread, filled with frustration as we watched and heard the uneven attack continue. Robert pleaded for help, bees clinging to the veil and crawling over his coveralls. We couldn't open the door and allow him to enter because we knew the bees would come with him, would follow him by the thousands, would attack those in the cottage, and we had no protective clothing, nothing to cope with such a calamity.

"Grab me that can of insect spray!" I shouted.

I grabbed the can, opened the door just wide enough to get my hand out, and tossed the container to Robert.

The air was filled with the nauseating insecticide as he swept it around his head, down over his body and around his feet, winning a brief respite from the angry squadron of bees. As he continued his spray attack and the bees gave him room to manoeuvre he edged closer to the cottage door. I stood ready to open it quickly when the opportunity presented itself as Robert seemed to be gaining some ground. I snapped the door open and he stumbled through, closing it on his heels, dead and dying bees dropping from his coveralls. The few bees that were successful in gaining entry with him were soon disposed of by fly-swatter, rolled newspapers and magazines and insecticide spray. The battle was over and the bees had won.

The buzzing squadron outside didn't do a victory roll and leave, either. For more than an hour after Robert's rescue, the angry drone of the honey bees kept us in a state of near panic as they circled the cottage relentlessly, probing for a breach in our defences. Finally, either their anger abated or they decided they'd better get back to their nectar and pollen gathering chores, and the bees departed from the cottage area.

Robert was in bad shape. He had been stung scores of times. The bees had managed to find chinks in his armor of protective netting and openings in his clothing that they were able to sneak through. The blue coveralls had hundreds of small black barbed arrows protruding from the material, the stingers of the bees. They're still there as the protective clothing hangs from a nail in the barn, mute testimony to the danger of angry bees.

When Robert undressed, his body was covered with stings, angry red bumps on his face, neck, arms, legs, torso and other parts of his body. He spent the next week in bed on special medication as he recovered from the terrifying experience.

"It was my own fault," he later explained. "The smoker went out and I continued working at the hive. I should have taken time to relight the bark. I was warned by other beekeepers that this could happen if I didn't maintain the smoke. It keeps the bees quiet."

That was the end of the beekeeping experiment at Twin Pines Farm, but it wasn't the end of the bees. They're still making their daily rounds during the summer months and it's a good thing they are. Our apple and cherry trees, our berries and vegetables depend on bees for pollination, just as the bees depend on them for nectar and pollen. Anyone wanting to risk getting stung at the farm need only go near the large patch of thyme growing on our rock garden slope. It is literally covered with honey bees and bumblebees when the lavender flowers appear.

Bumblebees are of the genus *Bombus*. They say the bumblebees in Carleton County are as large as canaries, so huge they can be seen coming from a long distance off and can be shot down with a .22 rifle. They are big and they have created numerous incidents at the farm, mainly because of their lifestyle. Bumblebees have a queen, workers and drones but they don't live in man-made hives. They seem to prefer our woodpiles at the farm.

The bumblebee is not really a belligerent insect and will leave people and animals alone unless provoked. The problem comes with their interpretation of provocation. If they have created a home in a woodpile and people shift the pile or start adding more wood, with no intention of disturbing the bees, the bumblies often take this as a sign of provocation. The sound of angry bumblebees is something you don't want to hear.

We've heard it a few times as we were forced to destroy nests of bumblebees because of their location. One time they were behind a stack of fireplace wood close to the house, but they had crawled up under the lowest piece of siding and made a home. We decided we'd have to get them out of there as they were only a few feet from a door of the house and foot traffic was pretty heavy in the area. They were a danger that couldn't be ignored with children playing around the lawn only a few feet away.

Bees Are Buzzing!

We used the water hose method of attack, directing a jet up under the siding to flush out the nest, keeping a close eye on the comings and goings of the busy bees. We knew if we could get the nest out with the queen bee that we would have the problem solved. When the hay nest was flushed out it was thrown over the slope between the upper and lower lawns and we went about the business of cleaning up the mess and repiling the wood we had torn down to get at the bees. Grandsons Marshall and Douglas were playing around the area, our early warning system for returning bees.

Suddenly there was a terrified cry from Doug who was sitting at the edge of the lawn near the top of the slope. I rushed over and could see a large bumblebee on his face near an eye. No wonder he was terror stricken!

As I reached over, intending to brush the bee from his face, Doug jerked his head into the path of my descending hand. The bee certainly got brushed off but young Doug took quite a slap to the face, one that would leave him with black eyes and a swollen nose, compounded by the fact that the bee managed to get in a very painful sting before being "brushed off." My heroics in disposing of the bumblebee were not appreciated at the time, either by Doug or others who gathered around the caterwauling lad. It was an adventure still often discussed.

There have been other bee incidents at the farm, none as tragic in outcome as those previously mentioned. There is always the potential for a confrontation with honey bees or bumblebees, often with painful consequences. They are one of the hazards familiar to country living. Yet as I gaze out the baywindow of the living room my eyes are drawn to the creeping bed of thyme at the lower side of the rock garden. The dainty flowers are covered with bees of various sizes, busy at work, doing their thing in their own way, unafraid, concentrating only on harvesting nectar and pollen. They are a vital link in the bionomics chain and Twin Pines Farm would not be the same without them.

5
Metamorphosis: A House Emerges

Bees or no bees, Twin Pines Farm became "home" over the next couple of years, despite the fact that we had purchased a very nice property on Parklyn Court in Fredericton and my work kept me in Elm City much of the time. Trips to the farm were frequent, including most weekends, such holidays as we managed to get free, and vacations. It was no hardship living in Fredericton. I have visited many countries in my lifetime, travelled coast to coast in Canada a number of times, toured many of the states in the U.S. and lived for six years in one of them. Fredericton was and is our favorite city, the most beautiful, the most friendly, with always something to do, and we appreciated the cultural benefits of living in New Brunswick's capital.

Still, the siren song of Twin Pines Farm became more insistent, urging us to cast off our urban lifestyle and turn to the calm and tranquility of our rural "home." The spirit was certainly willing but there were practical concerns, centred around financial circumstances at the time and what the future would demand. It was time to get out pencils and paper and do some serious figuring.

Our long range plan indicated that the time had come to think about building a house at Twin Pines Farm, one that would serve us for the rest of our natural lives. The process began with Kay and I obtaining many magazines featuring different styles, shapes and sizes of houses. We visited model homes, thought seriously of erecting a log structure, even went so far as to pay seventy-five dollars for complete blueprints for a big A-frame home. We sharpened pencils, worked out costs, and the bottom line always came out the same: too expensive for our budget. We were fortunate in one way: our three children were grown and out on their own. We didn't need a big place. Indeed, a smaller house would mean less cost in the beginning and lower maintenance in future years. We changed our line of thinking, putting aside those impractical dreams of the perfect home that would be a look-alike of hundreds and thousands of other magazine picture homes.

"Why not go with what we have," I suggested one night as we stopped for a cup of coffee, dejected after studying dozens of home plans and working out costs.

"What do you mean 'go with what we have'?" Kay snapped, understandably irritated after an evening of frustration. "We can't live in a cottage for the rest of our lives. You'd freeze to death, if nothing worse."

She was stating what should have been obvious: the cottage had no insulation and, sitting on cement blocks, the wind whistled around, over and under the building.

"You're right," I replied soothingly. "What I meant was to take the cottage we have and use it as a starting point for a future home. We'd have a basement dug, cement walls poured, then move the cottage onto that solid foundation. That would give us a two storey house."

Kay sipped her coffee as she contemplated what I had said. It was an idea we hadn't considered to that time and there was no guarantee that it could be done. But was it worth a try? I sat back and waited as Kay thought of the possibilities. The metamorphosis of our cottage into a dream home would be an accomplishment rivalling that of the most exotic butterfly.

Finally Kay smiled at me, neither an affirmation nor a denial. "Let's sleep on it, Jim. Perhaps it can work."

When I came home from work the next night Kay had a surprise waiting: plans for both floors of a two storey house, based on the dimensions of our cottage. "It will take a lot of work and more planning," she said, "and we'll probably make changes as we go along but I believe it can be done."

I looked at her drawings and nodded in agreement. She and our son Bruce had done an amazing job of moving partitions around, of creating space, and the suggestions for the basement area were practical. I suggested a few changes but nothing major. The finished product was to be much as Kay and Bruce had planned it, a complete transformation of the cottage that had given us so many happy days. There was much to do before the cottage underwent any changes. The building was strictly a summer place with no insulation, thin panel partitions blocking off living cubes, no running water, only a chemical toilet, no bathtub, no shower, no electricity. We had to find a builder, explain what we planned, determine if it was feasible and, finally, decide if we could afford to proceed with construction. If it was going to be too costly we would have to put the project on the back burner. We wanted the building to be close to the location of the original farmhouse, on the ridge that gave a spectacular view up and down the St. John River.

We were told that the plan was reasonable, that the cottage could be moved from its cement block base to a solid cement foundation. Earth-moving equipment would be brought in to dig the foundation, cement walls poured, then the building moved on rollers to its new base. The builder assured us that he could do the job within our proposed budget. There would be no outlay for land, and he could see no obstacles that would change the picture.

The biggest obstacle for us at the time was the money. By selling our house in Fredericton we would have enough equity to finance a portion of the cost of changing the cottage into a full-time, all-weather house. A mortgage would handle the rest, if such could be arranged. There were frustrating delays, mountains of paper work both in Fredericton and Woodstock.

The builder was given the green light to proceed with construction. We visited the farm as often as possible during the building stage, a lot of trips between Fredericton and Wakefield. Every weekend was reserved for being at the farm and visits were made at nights during the week. Kay sometimes stayed with Beth and Robert in Woodstock so as to be able to be at the farm when decisions had to be made, and to keep a close eye on progress. We had rented an apartment in Fredericton until such time as we could move into the house at the farm, as my work at The Daily Gleaner and The Atlantic Advocate demanded a great deal of my time.

The first major problem the builder faced came during excavation for the lower storey. The idea was to build the first storey into the side hill, resulting in three sides of the cement foundation walls being enclosed by solid earth, only the side facing east being open. The bad news was that the earth moving equipment had struck solid rock and the excavation could not be as deep as was intended. The good news was that the cement walls and floor would be on a solid base of rock. Earth fill could be used to cover the cement walls on the north, south and west sides. The other option was to use explosives to remove rock and the increased cost of the foundation would then throw our budget out of kilter. We decided there was nothing wrong with having our dream house built on solid rock; it had a nice touch of symbolism.

The cement walls looked stark and bare when the foundation was poured, gaps allowing space for a door and windows on the east side and a small window near the top of the wall on the south side. The floor was poured cement. We worried if the cottage would sit on the foundation properly, fretted that measurements were wrong, that the building would either fall into the basement or settle over the outside walls. Moving the cottage was quite a feat involving men and machines but finally the building sat high and snug on its new footing.

Some have been critical of locating the house where we did, more than a hundred yards downhill from Route 103. Most homes in the area are built closer to the highway with the front door facing the road. We had no desire to have our home facing fields and a busy highway, not when we had the St. John River flowing by our property and a spectacular valley hill on the other side, assuring that we could watch the sun come up every day there was a cloudless sky. Our decision was to have the so-called front door face the highway but the "real" front of the building would face east. After the cottage was in place on its newly poured walls we could see that our choice was right. Looking down from the highway you see a small one-storey bungalow with a central door and small windows on either side. It doesn't look like much of a house, seemingly small and cramped, with no saving graces. Looks can be deceiving.

The home at Twin Pines Farm, when seen from the river side or from Route 105 across the valley, is a two-storey structure with a deck running the full length of the house on the east side. Large glass patio doors give access to the deck from the living room. The front of the house is at the back, and the back at the front. That's the way we wanted it and that's the way it is. Those who take the trouble to drive down to the house and see the view we have from the deck quickly understand why we built the house backwards, so to speak. We gained a lot of pleasure and comfort by flaunting tradition when we decided on the location of the building.

Once the cottage was on its new site the builder and his crew were able to get down to the serious work of the transformation of the cottage into a home. An electric line was run downhill from Route 103 to give the carpenters electricity to power their tools. Gone are the days of exclusive use of hand saws, planes, hammer and nails — and endless hours of hard labor. Electric table saws were moved on to the site to go along with portable power saws, electric drills and even power hammers. One of the major cost items in today's world is labor, so any labor-saving devices that can be employed result in financial savings. That's certainly true in theory but time saved by the use of high-tech tools is often wasted if workers have to wait around for the builder to show up and give new orders.

The first challenge was to tackle the interior of the cottage, tearing down the partitions and leaving nothing but a shell with a roof. Some of the paneling was rescued to be used for the walls of the utility room that would have a washer-dryer, hot water tank, deep sink, and room for a deep freezer and shelving for canned preserves, jams, jellies and pickles. Then came the job of erecting the new partitions for the upper storey to follow Kay's plans for a bedroom, half-bath, kitchen, dining area and living room. Changes had to be made in the exterior walls of the south and west sides to accommodate a large picture window looking east, double glass patio-doors that would exit from the living room onto the deck, and a bow window facing directly south. All of that glass was designed to give the house an open, bright look; it also resulted in a panoramic view from the dining area and living room that still draws gasps of wonder from new visitors to Twin Pines Farm.

One decision we took certainly added to the breaking of our budget at that time, though it probably saved money in the long run. We wanted the cabinets in the kitchen to be hand made, not a look-alike of those available from building supplies showrooms. We wanted our kitchen to have a different appearance. This would require the services of a cabinetmaker. We were fortunate. There was a skilled carpenter in the building crew who was also a cabinetmaker.

Having such an expert there, it didn't take much imagination to decide that he should also build closets in both the half-bath upstairs and the full-bath below. Provision for a closet in the upper level bedroom conveniently left room for a dresser. Why not have the cabinet maker build a dresser into that good space, and perhaps some shelving above? Why not, indeed. What resulted from this proposal was a combination dresser, wide writing desk and bookshelf.

We put another dent in our carefully prepared budget when it came time to choose the wood for these special projects. Gary Marsten, the man who was going to do the actual work, offered a number of options. It was love at first sight when we were shown a red cedar veneer sample and the decision for the kitchen cabinets came quickly, even though the cedar was one of the more expensive alternatives. We made up for that slightly by choosing less expensive birch for the bathroom and bedroom cabinets. We were tremendously pleased with the excellent work done by Gary. The red cedar cabinets in the kitchen still give us a great deal of pleasure and are the topic of conversation when first-time visitors step through the door. The kitchen is small and shaped like an open-ended rectangle but Kay had marvelous insight in drawing the plan. Everything is within easy reach.

Gary's fine handiwork resulted in kitchen-cabinet work that would be appealing in any glossy magazine featuring colorful furniture. There are hanging cabinets over the sink, stove and refrigerator on the west side, and on the south end of the kitchen wall. Built-in cabinets and drawers on three sides are topped with arborite working space.

There were other impulsive ideas that were to add to the strain on our tight budget. For example, we opted for more than the usual number of electric outlets in each room, having lived in too many homes and apartments where it was often difficult to locate an outlet. We've never been sorry for the decision but it did add to the cost at the time.

So did my obsession with fireplaces. We had purchased an antique Franklin-type stove some years before and I wanted it built into the den-library-office in the lower level. This small cast iron stove was built to burn coal but could also handle wood. My decision to have it built in meant that the chimney would have to be double the width needed for the average fireplace, and twice the height, as we also wanted a fireplace in the living room. This added not only to the labor bill but also the cost of materials. Battering of the budget, in this instance, was not the fault of the builder. It was proof of the old adage: champagne taste and a beer purse.

(We were to learn in time that the bricklayer had not understood the complexity of the Franklin in the basement, nor allowed for the height of the chimney and the fact that the stove was offset from the flue. The Franklin couldn't be used: when a fire was lighted the room immediately filled with smoke. Years later part of the chimney above the Franklin had to be torn down and reconstructed to achieve a proper draw of air and eliminate the smoke problem.)

We received another shock when the well-driller arrived and set up his rig. We expected he would find water very quickly since we knew we already had a well about fifteen feet deep only a hundred or so feet up hill, and had dug our own sweet water spring only fifty feet down hill. All went smoothly with the first length of drill, the bit biting through the ground as though it were butter. The problem came with the second section.

"We've hit solid rock at nineteen feet," the driller informed me. I had taken a few days off from work because I wanted to see how a water well was drilled.

"Is that good news or bad?" I asked.

"Well, the good news is that we won't have to insert pipe where we are drilling through solid rock because it makes its own rock pipe, and that could be a saving," he explained. "On the other hand, it will take longer to drill through solid rock and quite often in these cases it means a deeper well."

He was right on both counts. It did take longer and he had to drill and drill and drill. I would sit and watch, smoking nervously, as the bit was hauled up and yet another section of drill pipe added. The drill reached 285 feet before a proper water table was struck.

"We're still not getting as good a flow as we should have," the driller said. "I'm going to have to bring in the thumper to break it up down there."

It worked. Now the plumber could go ahead with hooking up his water supply to bathrooms, kitchen, outside tap, and laundry area. An immersible pump was lowered 200 feet down the well, attached to a pressure pump, and soon the water was flowing. We still marvel that such a comparatively small pump could continue to supply us water year after year with no problems.

Work on the house itself continued at what seemed to me to be a snail's pace. Insulation was placed in the walls and in the attic. Rooms were walled. Siding was added to the exterior of the house. Ceilings were installed, except in the utility area on the bottom floor. We had decided on electric heating with each room having its own thermostat and this was done. Picture and bow windows were in place, as well as other windows, as were the sliding, heavy glass patio-doors. The deck was in place and ran the full length of the house on the east side.

The house was almost finished. Our budget had been finished for several weeks now. The builder had underestimated and we had insisted on frills that drove up the costs.

"We're at a dead end," I said unhappily, as Kay and I discussed our plight. "I don't want to add to the mortgage, to borrow more money, for that would put a crimp in our long range plans to have this place free of debt by the time we retire."

"What we can do, Jim, is to tell the builder that we no longer need his men, that we've completed as much as we are going to do at this time. The house is livable now and we can do much of the work ourselves."

The decision was made. There would be quite a bit to do as we were to find out very quickly. All of the rooms had to be painted, though the walls had been prepared and given a primer coat of white. There were no floor coverings, except in the kitchen. Ceiling tiles had to be put up in the utility room. There was much to do but we had lots of time to do it. We had for all practical purposes achieved a major part of our long range planning for retirement.

The summer cottage had metamorphosed into an all season home. Now the fun began!

6
Cleaning Up Loose Ends

The metamorphosis was far from complete, both inside the house and the exterior. It was a mess: scraps of building materials, from wood to insulation, were a blight to the eyes. Much of the scrap lumber could be salvaged for use in the fireplaces. Other material had to be hauled to the dump. Son Bruce, who had been of tremendous help during construction, remained a strong supporter of the project, both in spirit and in action.

We appreciated both his good ideas and his physical strength because there was planning to do and many jobs that required hard labor. There was no lawn, just a yard of gravel and earth surrounding the house, and this desert itself surrounded by fields. The driveway had been graded, as was the yard, with the fill being levelled to the house. We made the decision then that we would not have a formal lawn or lawns; we would have an old fashioned yard of grass, weeds and anything else that would grow.

However, even a yard requires attention. We did have to apply lime and fertilizer and a mixture of seeds to get something growing in that desert. We ended up with two poor excuses for lawns; one is quite large and surrounds the house, the second being at a lower level and separated from the upper one by a steep slope.

The lower lawn, a mixture of grass and sturdy weeds, was special to us because an old apple tree stands on the north edge just twenty feet from the house. It is a resting place for birds of many species.

The lawns get mowed frequently but have never been given the care and attention to become textbook pictures. Their saving grace is that they are green, if it rains sufficiently during the summer. They're also mighty pretty when the dandelions are in bloom because these yellow wildflowers grow in profusion at Twin Pines Farm. We make no effort to eradicate them.

The only weed we have declared war on is the burdock. Kay hates them with a passion and her annual battle is always a losing one. The Scotch thistles offer a challenge we have never accepted; they're beautiful, so why not let them grow. Other weeds, some colorful and some drab, are tolerated — except in the garden and the flower beds. Our concern has almost always been to let nature take her course at Twin Pines Farm, to place trees, flowers and weeds where she wants them. We have retained veto rights, of course, and Kay continues her yearly battle with burdocks while I worry about the spread of the red willow.

We actually thought we could and would control nature on the farm when we first started planning. We would remove all of the alders, we would control weeds and shrubs, we would manicure the landscape until it rated publicity in one of the glossy "home and country" type magazines.

Oh, what dreams we had: trails for horseback riding and walks through the woods, badminton and/or tennis courts, horseshoe pitches, a lawn bowling green, a swimming pool, possibly a boat landing or two along the river, plantations of trees, orchards of apples and plums, a vineyard. There were endless possibilities.

Bruce manfully tackled the problem of alders, with axe and chain saw. Down they went by the hundreds, huge piles of this common weed tree. We were quick to learn that it is not sufficient to merely cut alders down. If you want to get rid of them you must dig out the roots or they'll just grow back again. They did, and have expanded their territory since our first futile effort to control them.

We had nothing against alders as such, of course, but did have visions of plantations of Christmas trees at Twin Pines Farm, both as a provider of an annual income after retirement and to improve the cosmetics of the property. The first thousand seedlings we obtained were planted by Bruce in a straight line for a quarter of a mile along the highway side of the property, with enough remaining to extend several hundred yards down the north side.

There were several problems with this strategy. First, we were turned down for a supply of trees the following year because we had not followed regulations in the first instance. They should have been planted in a one acre plot with specified distances between the trees and the rows. Secondly, planting the trees along the edge of the property proved to be a disaster when a careless motorist threw a burning cigarette butt from his vehicle one spring and this started a grass fire. The flames destroyed quite a few of the trees, leaving large gaps. Those remaining are now three times as tall as Christmas trees and do give us some measure of privacy from passing motor traffic.

Having learned our lesson from our first experience, Robert and I decided we'd have another try. We were able to obtain a thousand trees after drawing up a proper plan and explaining what we intended. This time we measured off the acre of land, drove stakes and strung line to mark off rows of the proper width and identified the location where each tree was to be planted. This huge grid soon became a Christmas tree plantation, a small one but a start. After the tender care of feeding and pruning for a few years the trees had grown well and we had a very neat looking acre plantation, a textbook picture. Then came a second fire. That year, however, the upper fields were not ploughed, providing a sort of firebreak. They were, instead, parched stubble and clumps of tinder-dry straw and the flames soon roared across the fields, at one time endangering the house.

Fortunately, the fire didn't reach the house but it did sweep through the dry grass to the Christmas tree plantation and left only a few trees untouched. That was the end of the Christmas tree project. Our plan to plant at least ten acres in spruce and fir was abandoned.

That doesn't mean we gave up entirely on tree planting but we no longer sought to do so as an income-producing project. Since that disastrous fire we have planted plum trees, a variety of dwarf apple trees, cherry trees, spruce, fir, tamarack, juniper and pine. Grandson Marshall once brought home a large number of red pine seedlings that he planted in a north meadow above the tree line and below the cultivated fields.

Raising trees in the country is a much tougher job than it is in the city, we were quick to discover. Porcupines occupied Twin Pines Farm for hundreds of years before we arrived. They still do and they find young trees a real taste treat during the winter months when snow makes it easy to reach the tree tips. They had quite a feast in Marshall's red pine grove and there are some mighty strange look- ing trees in that particular meadow today. Field mice also leave their marks during the winter months, tunneling under the snow to chew at the tender bark, seeming to prefer young fruit trees. They will completely circle a trunk, removing the bark and thus causing the death of the tree in most instances. We have lost some plantings to mice but have been able to save a few.

We quickly learned to use guards to protect the trunks of young trees but even so we still have problems. Despite the presence of hawks and other predatory birds, Twin Pines Farm has a tremendous population of field mice. They've managed to infiltrate the house on several occasions to take up winter quarters but, so far, we've managed to win those battles. The war is not yet won.

Cleaning up loose ends took several years. We still spent a lot of time exploring the forty-five acres, taking special satisfaction in roaming through the woods, marvelling at the variety of trees, flowers and shrubs that we found. We were impressed with the size of two huge maple trees, each hundreds of years old, that still stood at different locations. One of these still had live branches and the remains of a tree house built by some youngster of a previous owner of the farm. This tree was surrounded by a grove of young maples and though the ancient maple has since returned to dust, its offspring keep growing, living memorials to the giant maple syrup producer. Part of the tremendous trunk of the other old maple still stands. This ancient marvel was the inspiration for the magic tree in my book *Foxy Freddy's Bicentennial Party* and I'm afraid the book will outlast the tree, though it will not have as long a life as that old maple. We often wonder how many hundreds of gallons of sap those old trees provided during their many decades of living.

We were still going back and forth between Fredericton and Wakefield, a combination of apartment living and country home. At first I attempted to commute, a drive of about eighty miles in the morning and the same at night. It was too much for me, stretching my hours to intolerable lengths, though I have friends who did it for years. We decided on a less stressful solution. I drove to Fredericton Monday mornings, checked into the apartment and then went to work. I'd drive up to Wakefield Wednesday evening after work, spend the night, then drive back to Elm City Thursday mornings accompanied by Kay. This gave her a couple of days to visit friends, shop and take care of business. We would return to Twin Pines Farm Friday night unless I had to remain in the city for some special reason.

This was a good arrangement for me, the best of both worlds. It also meant that Kay performed the lion's share of cleaning up loose ends at the farm, both inside the house and outdoors. She was probably just as happy. There was a lot of painting to be done and I'm the sloppiest man with a paint brush ever to have served in the Canadian navy. Kay also had to hang curtains and drapes, oversee the laying of carpets after choosing color and design, try to make do with a minimum of furniture, much of what we had being used in the apartment. She took charge of finances, arranged insurance for cars and home, cooked, put up preserves, jams and jellies, and did the thousands of other things that must be done to make Twin Pines Farm a viable retirement home.

The lure of the farm became so intense that I had no choice but to take an early retirement from full time daily newspaper work. I couldn't really afford such a step, as I soon discovered, because there was so much to be done at the farm, plus my impulsive drive to do even more, including purchase of machinery and erection of some outbuildings. Two of the gifts I received from staff and management at *The Daily Gleaner* and *The Atlantic Advocate* when I retired were a fine fishing rod, reel and line, and a chain saw. I hoped to spend many hours with that fishing rod because that's my favorite sport. It turned out that I spent considerably more time with the chain saw.

Kay had cleaned up most of the loose ends by the time I retired for the first time. My head was filled with dreams of trout fishing, creating a garden, constructing outbuildings to house tools and machinery, starting a vineyard, adding livestock and poultry to the operation, getting wood for the fireplaces. There was no end to the list of things to do.

7

Country Carpenter, eh?

Country carpenters have built this nation, as they did the United States, men and women who had, or developed, the skills necessary to erect homes, barns and other buildings in the rural areas of North America. No professional carpenters were available, no electricians, no plumbers, no dry wall experts or painters. When it comes to country carpentry, I'm a klutz (as I am at most tasks that demand manual skills). That doesn't mean that I don't try. Oh how I have tried, and tried and tried! I've suffered the mashed thumbs, cuts and bruises often enough to prove that carpentry is not my field.

I was determined to escape my reputation as a klutz at manual skills by learning to be a carpenter at Twin Pines Farm. There were projects that had to be done if we were to get into farming in even a small way. I knew that I was helpless with a hammer, that I couldn't drive a nail without bending it. I knew I had absolutely no skill with a hand saw, that my straight line cuts all ended up as majestic curves.

Putting a carpenter's level in my hands was akin to handing a sextant to a lumberjack and asking him to "shoot the sun." Pliers, screwdrivers, wrenches, planes, sawhorses and nail pullers were in my vocabulary as a writer but were foreign to me as a would-be carpenter. I had a lot to learn and I was fortunate that Robert was available to be my tutor and my chief carpenter. The first project on the list would be a barn so we could get tools and machinery out of the weather. We drew up a rough diagram of a building that could be built in stages, one that would eventually give us four separate rooms. "We can build it on the old barn foundation north of the house," I suggested.

"Man, we're not going to build any barn ninety feet long," Robert replied, "you'll never be doing that much farming."

I agreed. "But we will have livestock some time down the road, and chickens, and we'll need a dry place for hay and straw and grain," I argued.

It was decided we would build only part of the barn that year. It would be straight up to the peak on the north side, with the roof sloping south to a lower wall, giving us two rooms.

The next year we planned to build an addition the same size on the north. Eventually we were to add a wing on both north and south sides. The first structure would have a work bench built along the east wall with a window to give some light, a necessity as our workshop would have no electricity.

We soon discovered we had made a mistake in laying out the design. We misjudged where the first section should go and left ourselves with no cement foundation for the south wing when its time came. It has never come.

A trip to Maritime Lumber Limited paid off with delivery of a truck load of two-by-fours and boards. Hemlock. Rough hemlock. We deliberately chose this wood because of its long-life quality and we chose rough hemlock because of price. We quickly learned that when you purchase rough (unplaned) lumber your two-by-fours are at least that, sometimes more. Your one-by-eight boards are at least that, often more. Quite a few of the boards were a foot wide and some as much as sixteen feet long. We also learned something else about hemlock: if you get a splinter in your hand the wound will start festering almost at once. There were many splinters before that summer was over because rough lumber guarantees there will be many wounds. Sturdy gloves were a help, of course, but there are times when something must be done without gloves, or they are forgotten, and the miniature poison-tipped daggers are just waiting for a chance to jab into a finger, hand or arm — and don't sit on a piece of rough hemlock.

We were amazed when the load of lumber was delivered. What would we do with all of those studs and boards and oversized two-by-fours? There seemed to be too much. The pile of green hemlock presented a challenge we were not sure we could meet, boards varying in width and length, some studs eight feet long and some twelve.

"We'll have to sort this pile," Robert suggested, "like putting all ten foot by eight inch boards in one pile and so on. Then we can just go to the right pile when we need a specific size. It'll save a lot of sawing."

It didn't save any sweat, though. Doing an inventory of the lumber pile and stacking it according to size took the best part of a day. It was hot, back-breaking work. The green wood was heavier than expected, the long pieces awkward to handle. It was not a job to be done without the use of sturdy gloves. However, when boards and studs had been separated into stacks by size it did seem that we had brought order out of chaos, that we could proceed with easier access to the lumber we needed.

"Where do we go from here?" I asked, completely ignorant as to how to start to construct a building. I had vague notions of building the frames of walls on the ground and then raising them to stand on the cement foundation.

"When we start tomorrow we begin with the framing," Robert explained, "but I don't think we can prefabricate the frames flat on the ground and then raise them. They'd be too heavy. You had enough trouble with one long board." We started off the next morning using hand saws. Robert could make a straight cut with no problem at all, using a carpenter's square to draw his lines. That didn't help me. No matter how straight the pencilled line, I ended up with a curve at the end of the board or stud. Hand sawing proved to be hard work and time consuming. We were making slow progress.

A very long extension cord strung from the house to the barn site solved the problem, and speeded up the work, as Robert was able to bring his power saw into play. I felt even more a klutz when I discovered that I couldn't make a straight cut even when using a power saw. My role as assistant to the head carpenter was relegated to that of a gopher — go for a piece of lumber, go for a fresh jug of water (or can of beer), go for some nails or spikes, go for a roll of tar paper, go for the blue chalk line. I'm an excellent gopher.

Hemlock is a difficult material to work with, especially green hemlock. In addition to its proclivity to inflict poisonous wounds, it warps badly and quickly as it dries. This was soon evident in the number of twisted studs and walls as we framed the building. The air was often blue around the site as we tried to find true pieces of stud to lay on the cement as the bottom of the wall frames. It became even more difficult as we struggled to raise the vertical two-by-fours. We later discovered that some pieces that were straight when built into the frame would twist hideously as they dried out and would have to be replaced, or another one added to the frame for strength.

Finally the frame was up and the walls and roof boarded. Getting the four walls framed was hard work but adding the trusses to support a roof called on courage I didn't realize I had. I must have been born with acrophobia.

I recalled how I broke out in a cold sweat during the Second World War when I was told to climb the free-swinging ladder to the crow's nest and stand lookout. I did what I was told. I also did what Robert said I must, clamber astride the top of those shaky wall frames and help him spike the joists in place. I must admit that the more joists added, the firmer the structure became, or so it seemed. I sweated gallons as we worked only twelve feet above the ground, most of the perspiration caused by my fear of height.

Construction of the trusses to form the roof line took me to even greater heights, the peak being about five feet above the joists. There was a lot of climbing up and down for the gopher and for Robert as measurements were taken and pieces of two-by-four had to be cut to specific lengths with the ends angled to fit precisely. Perhaps it is taking liberties with the language to use the word "precisely" in the context of building our barn. There are a number of gaps that indicate that we were either wrong in measuring our angles, or we goofed in sawing the wood. These small aberrations, not serious enough to keep us from going ahead with the job, can probably be blamed on the fact that I sometimes forsook my gopher role and tried my hand with the electric saw.

There are no photographs to record for posterity those sweaty days when we struggled to erect the joists and trusses for the barn.

Too bad. I provided comic relief for Robert, and for Kay, Beth, Marshall and Doug as I fought to maintain my grip atop the framing, both legs wrapped tightly around the rough studding, holding on fiercely with one hand while I attempted to help Robert put a joist or truss in place. My productivity improved as I became more used to the situation but I had not overcome my acrophobia, nor have I to this day.

We thought we had built the framing, joists and trusses solidly until we casually leaned against one of the sides while taking a rest — and it leaned with us. The addition of a number of strategically placed braces seemed to fix the problem. The building took on added strength as we nailed the hemlock boards to the four walls, and completely boarded over the roof. We pushed and shoved and tugged, adding more braces to the framing as we found weak spots.

The addition of expensive aluminum roofing promised (but did not deliver) a dry building inside. We were proud of that first effort. Robert proved he was a good country carpenter, a quick learner. I proved acceptable as a gopher. Even so, I had learned a great deal about construction during the summer and although I lacked the skills of a carpenter, I was no longer afraid to tackle some maintenance jobs. My knowledge of carpentry and the use of tools increased immeasurably; my mechanical skills showed only slight progress.

It was the following spring before we learned of another mistake we had made. The hemlock building sat nicely on its cement foundation until the high winter winds struck that solid, flat north

side. We have fierce winds at Wakefield and over the long winter the force was enough to move the building half a foot off the foundation on the south side. We introduced several new words to the language as we struggled to move the building back where it belonged. Eventually we had to borrow some house jacks to lift the south side of the building. Then we used our pickup to push against the building and finally it settled in its rightful place. We located spikes that could be driven through the base of the framing into the cement, thus securing the building solidly to the foundation.

Another load of rough hemlock arrived at the site and we prepared for the second phase of construction. We had both learned valuable lessons during our tutorial year of the first phase and the second summer saw us moving ahead more quickly, with fewer mistakes. At the end of the season we had a good sized building with three rooms, a large one in the middle with walls separating it from the ones on the north and south sides. This time we decided to save money when it came time to put a roof on the new addition. There must be something that would be less costly than the fabricated aluminum. Penny wise, pound foolish.

We decided to "shingle" the roof of the new part of the building using old aluminum photo offset plates from *The Bugle* in Woodstock, obtained easily and at a "bargain" price. They were covered with black printers' ink and it wasn't long before Robert and I were in the same condition, hands, face and clothing. These metal plates are thin but we felt they would serve the purpose well if we first laid tar paper on the roof and used the proper nails. This we did. The roof leaked like a sieve. We purchased a large can of roofing tar and made an effort to seal each and every hole where water might seep in. This solution worked during light rains; a heavy storm and we had water dripping from the ceiling and rafters. Eventually we were forced to apply proper aluminum roofing on the north side, the same as we used on the south. Now we are bothered with a leaky roof only during the most severe storms.

We were much more successful in battling leaks when we built the poultry house, more commonly known as a hen house. We attached it to the east side of the barn building with its own door. We wanted a place that would house comfortably up to thirty laying hens, and maybe a rooster or two. Being thoughtful farmers, we erected two chicken-wire yards for the poultry to get their daily exercise: one had an entry-exit on the north side of the building, an area that received the early morning sun but was shaded and cool in the afternoon; the other entry-exit was on the south side, where the sun shone from morning until sunset.

Though constructed mainly of scrap lumber and aluminum roofing left over, we took pride in this future home for whatever poultry we might obtain. It was well ventilated, had plenty of light from a window in the south end, had good rough-board flooring well above the ground, and presented few problems from water leaks during storms. Some of our large alders were used to build roosts for the hens. It proved to be a nice home for some rather unusual birds over the years.

That was not the end of my apprenticeship in country carpentry. In later years Robert and I were called upon to build a shelter for goats, a frail three-sided roofed structure of posts and aluminum siding, open to the east. It was merely a place for the animals to get out of the rain and/or sun while they were in the pasture. We built a similar but smaller three-sided roofed shelter in a tiny pasture the year we ranged a pair of pigs. Another building, a solid, peaked roof structure was located closer to the house, when we decided to raise a flock of meat hens, a winter's supply of chicken for the freezer.

Bruce proved his design and carpentry skills when he created and constructed a root cellar in the side hill below the upper lawn, just thirty paces or so from the east door of the house. He did most, if not all, of the work as well as planning the interior layout, including shelves and bins to hold the vegetables to be stored.

I proved that I'm just as big a klutz with a pick and shovel as I am with hammer and saw. A root cellar was almost a necessity when I was a tad living in Avondale. There were no freezers, no refrigerators, just ice boxes for homes. Most farms had an ice house to hold large blocks cut from nearby lakes and ponds during the winter months. Sawdust was used to keep the ice from melting. Root cellars were used to store carrots, turnips, cabbages, potatoes and other vegetables. Some were huge walk in cellars, such as the one at Kings Landing Historical Village. Others were small, as was the one designed by Bruce. He did a great job of building the cellar, with me playing the gopher role again, and he built shelves inside, as well as installing two ventilation pipes that thrust above ground. The door to the cellar was an insulated massive, heavy job designed to keep out both cold and air.

The root cellar was an artistic triumph and a practical disaster. Bruce had done his job well. So did Mother Nature when winter arrived. The slope was buried under many feet of snow every time we had a storm. It became nearly impossible to dig through packed drifts to open the door of the root cellar to get vegetables. The cellar's still there but it hasn't been used since the first winter after it was built. It is easier to store most vegetables in the freezer.

Country carpenter, eh? It has been fun and there are still challenges to be met.

8

Our Charley Chickens

Believe it or not, chickens do make wonderful pets that can be brought into the home and domesticated (to a degree). We first discovered this while living in a large, rambling 13-room home on Boyne Street in Woodstock when the children were young. We have the late, great Walter Tompkins to thank for this introduction to the pet world of chickens.

Walter was a legend in Carleton County and his death in 1988 was a tragic loss. We knew him from the time Radio CJCJ hit the air waves, where he became the "Voice of the Valley" with his regular farm reports, as well as his handling of newscasts. Always interested in farming, he was a pioneer in market gardening at his spread on Lockhart Mill road and became one of the prime strawberry producers in New Brunswick. He loved country music and gave many struggling artists their first steps up the ladder of success, both with his Open House stage shows, broadcast over CJCJ, and as the genial master of ceremonies at the annual country music competition during Old Home Week. He also instituted the annual Bluegrass Music and Strawberry Festival in Woodstock.

Carleton Country residents take great pride in the fact that Walter Tompkins was nominated to the New Brunswick Country Music Hall of Fame and was inducted as a member several years before his death. It was an honor he earned through promotion of singers, pickers, fiddlers and dancers.

There was another side to Walter, his empathy with children and his ability to earn their love and respect. I presume that is what happened the day sons Bruce and Ian came home with a baby chicken. Neither Kay nor I disapproved of chickens per se; we both had paid our dues gathering eggs, feeding and watering flocks, and cleaning hen houses. We did have our doubts about adopting a chicken while we lived in town.

"Where did you get that?" I asked when the boys brought the cheeping ball of yellow fluff into the house.

"Walter gave it to us," Bruce said proudly. His lower lip quivered as he asked, "We can keep it, Dad, can't we?"

I looked at Kay and saw that she was struggling to keep a straight face. I knew what her answer would have been and I wasn't about to become the heavy over a mere chicken. We'd cope someway.

"Well, I guess you can keep him — if you look after him," I said firmly. "You're to be in charge of the chicken, Bruce, and you'll have to find a place for him to live. He can't be kept in the house."

"Okay, Dad," Bruce agreed, a wide grin on his face. He and Ian scampered out the door with their new pet.

"Thanks a bunch, Walter," I growled to myself. "That chicken is going to cause us a lot of grief."

When I went outside a little later I found that a wooden packing crate had been commandeered by the boys to be used as a hen (or rooster house). At least that problem was solved.

"Have you named your pet yet?" I asked as we sat around the supper table.

"Charley. Charley Chicken," Bruce replied.

Charley had come into our lives and would make quite an impression on all of us. The rule was, of course, that the pet chicken was to be kept outside, that we didn't want him in the house. There was no way that we knew of that Charley could be potty trained and neither Kay nor I thought it feasible to put diapers on the feathered critter. Some say that rules are made to be broken. Whether that's so or not, it wasn't long before Charley became a part of the family, having the run of the downstairs part of the house as well as the yard. It is a scientific fact that baby chickens will respond to people and animals when first exposed to them, it is know as imprinting. Charley had become imprinted on us and had no fear of our dog, Brownie, nor of us. Though not housebroken, that little chicken made fewer mistakes than expected, not often enough to become a major problem and threaten his freedom to roam the house at will. He seemed to realize that going to the toilet was an outdoor activity. I often think about Charley Chicken. I can close my eyes and still hear his feet clicking on the floor as he ran from one room to another. He knew his name and would come when called. He loved to be picked up and cuddled, to be talked to, and craved attention. He became a family pet, fussed over by the boys, Beth, Kay and myself.

Charley was the only chicken, to my knowledge, that enjoyed watching television. In that old house the television was not kept in the living room or the parlor. It was located in the large downstairs hall, a room in itself, really. A couch took up space under the incline of the staircase to the second floor. When I found time in the evening to relax, you'd find me on the couch, watching television.

"Come, Charley," I would call. "Come to daddy."

Almost immediately the clicking feet of Charley would be heard as he trotted across the linoleum floor in the kitchen, through the hallway and into the television room. He would jump from the floor to my lap, curl up and watch the tube. However, Charley was a restless watcher. Perhaps he was bored with the commercials. Before long he would walk up my chest, climb onto a shoulder and cuddle in against my neck. If Charley had been a cat he would have purred but he did have his own sounds to let you know he was enjoying himself. We would both relax and suddenly I would feel a strange tingling in my ear. It would be Charley picking away at the hairs in the ear, causing a most uncomfortable sensation.

I'm sure that Beth and Kay and the boys had as much fun with Charley as I did, probably more, and he became a very important part of my busy and stress filled life.

Visitors to our home were amazed to hear that we had a chicken for a family pet. They were dumbfounded that we would allow him entry to the house. Their eyes started in disbelief when they witnessed Charley running when called and shocked when the bird settled in comfortably on my shoulder and then snuggled against my neck. They could understand my affinity for birds and animals, even those in the wild, but a pet chicken that was loved and cuddled and allowed to roam the house! Walter understood, though, and approved.

Then one day Charley Chicken disappeared, touching off a frenzied search, inside the house and out. We called his name as we roamed nearby streets and yards, around the old lumber supply complex. There was no response, no welcome clicking of feet on pavement in response to our entreaties for Charley to come home. We mourned our loss, as one grieves when something special is no longer part of your life — leaving nothing but pleasant memories.

It was years later that Charley Chicken II came into our lives, after the house was built at Twin Pines Farm and we had buildings to handle livestock. Bruce was responsible for the appearance of the second Charley, too.

Bruce decided to build his own incubator and hatch his own chickens. "Where can I build the incubator, Dad?" he asked. "It can't be in the barn because we have no electricity there."

Bruce knew as well as I did that there was only one place he could try his experiment: in the house. And there was only one logical place in the house: my combination den-library-office-bar. It had sufficient space for an incubator, had a number of electric outlets, was handy to a water supply as the bathroom was only feet away, had good ventilation with three windows that could be opened, and had electric heating if that should prove necessary after the chicks were born.

"I suppose you could use the den," I suggested with a grin, one that drew a parallel response from Bruce. "But we don't have an incubator and we can't afford to buy one right now, so what are you going to use?"

"I'll think of something," Bruce replied.

He did, too. He used a heat lamp that could be raised or lowered to retain the proper temperature for incubation. The average time before an egg hatches, under a hen or in an incubator, is twenty days and there must be a steady heat at a precise temperature reading. Bruce's Rube Goldberg contraption may have been primitive, compared to the high-tech electric incubators available today, but it was possible that it could be effective.

Our Charley Chickens

We had a few Araucanas — a special breed of combed, clean-legged Bantams. These are the famous Easter egg hens that produce blue-shelled eggs when not crossbred. When other blood lines are mixed with that of Araucanas the color of the eggs may still be blue, or green or even a green-khaki. It was Araucana eggs that Bruce wanted to hatch. He didn't know whether the eggs were fertile or not; that would be discovered when they were candled after eight or ten days in the incubator. There is more to hatching eggs than putting them in an incubator, giving them proper temperature, and waiting twenty days for a chick to appear. The eggs must be misted on a regular basis, they must be turned at proper intervals, and they must be protected against any wide swings in temperature. That's why many poultry fanciers prefer a broody hen over an incubator: the would-be mother's body supplies the necessary humidity to give moisture to the eggs under her, and she does the task of turning the eggs when she feels the time is right.

Bruce proved to be a good "mother," keeping a close watch on his incubating eggs, misting them, moving them, regulating the height of the heat lamp to maintain an even and correct temperature. He built a home-made candler to check the eggs about halfway through the incubation period, finding that quite a few of them were infertile.

Despite all of his efforts to keep a steady temperature in the incubator, there was trouble ahead. It was impossible to be in the hatching room all of the time and there were hours during the nights when no temperature checks were made. We all waited anxiously for the time when the chicks would start pipping their eggs. It usually takes twelve to twenty-four hours for the chick to break out of its shell after it first pecks a tiny hole in the shell of the egg.

There was great excitement the day Bruce thundered up the stairs and informed us that one egg was pipped. We all rushed to the hatching room and sure enough there was a small hole in one of the eggs. At least one chick was trying to make it all the way. What eventually emerged was a tiny brown-striped yellow ball of fluff. We had witnessed the first birth at Twin Pines Farm. Even our dog Molly seem pleased with this latest addition to the family.

Charley Chicken II became an integral part of our lives even more quickly than had the first Charley. Perhaps this was because he was an orphan, the only chick to survive that first attempt with a homemade incubator. More likely it was because he had a definite personality of his own.

We knew that Charley Chicken II was something special when Molly adopted him, a sight to remember. Molly was family and knew it. She would sprawl on the carpeted floor for hours, chin resting on the edge of the brooding pen, brown eyes following the quick steps of the chick as it darted around its courtyard. She never attempted to molest the tiny chick, nor did Charley show any fear of Molly. Charley Chicken II led a schizophrenic life, unable to decide whether he was a person or a dog. He was sure of one thing: he wasn't a chicken or a hen. He would have nothing to do with that noisy flock of feathered cousins.

Charley Chicken II grew into a beautiful rooster, with the reds, golds, yellows and browns so common to Araucanas. He would never deign to live in the henhouse or be cooped up in the poultry yard. He demanded, and got, his own home in the section of the barn used to stall cattle and/or goats. His appearance became more splendid as he grew older, developing an arrogant red comb with long, delicate red and gold feathers like a flowing mane from his head to shoulders. He was the king of the flock but refused his crown. Charley's world was one of people and a dog.

Our magnificent Araucana rooster never did become a steady household pet, though he was invited in from time to time and was closely watched. However, he earned full pet status. As soon as anyone went outdoors, Charley would appear and follow their footsteps, talking animatedly, his legs churning as he attempted to keep pace. If there were no people around, Charley would follow

Molly as she made her rounds of the farm marking her territorial imperative. The "rooster who wasn't" would respond to his name when called, just as the first Charley Chicken had. It was seldom necessary to call him because most of the time he appeared as soon as he heard a door open.

Charley Chicken II was good company. He had the range of the farm, clawing the ground looking for fresh food, strolling through garden and hay field to catch a quick snack. His was a life of bliss. He loved to be picked up, cuddled, talked to, stroked. He would hitchhike a ride, standing proudly on your shoulder as you walked around. He was also a practical joker and a nuisance at times. Kay spends a great deal of time in the garden, weeding, hoeing, grooming and fighting her eternal battle against burdocks. Charley wasn't much help in the gardening but he was usually there when Kay was working. During the harvesting season Kay would pick berries or other produce and place them in a container beside her and Charley would reach in, grab a berry and run away, Kay in hot pursuit. It became a regular game, one the rooster obviously enjoyed. As soon as she returned to her picking chores, Charley would sneak back, ready for another raid and run.

We never did know for sure if Charley had a girl friend. It would be a shame if his genes were lost to the poultry world. He was such a splendid rooster in appearance. He may have had a secret love life that we didn't know about. Although he was the only one of the feathered flock given free range, we did have occasions when hens and roosters made a jail break and won at least a temporary respite from their wire enclosed prison. Any farmer or rancher can tell you that fixing fencing and wire enclosures is a never ending job. If poultry and animals can't find escape holes, they'll make them. So it is entirely possible that Charley Chicken II did have a secret love life. He was one handsome rooster! Love them? Maybe. Live with them? Never! This refusal to be one of the flock, even if king, was Charley's Achilles' heel.

We knew something was wrong when Bruce returned to the house one extremely cold winter morning after feeding and watering the flock. The mercury had plunged deeply overnight and it was one of those mornings when the frigid air stung the nostrils. Bruce's eyes brimmed with tears as he came in the door, his face a mask of grief. "Charley's dead," he announced, his voice breaking.

My Adam's apple seemed to swell and block my throat as I fought against the anguish I felt. "What happened, Bruce?" I asked.

He explained that when we put some hens in with Charley in the stall barn, our proud rooster was most unhappy that he had to share his accommodations. The move had become necessary because the poultry house was too crowded and some of the pullets had been transferred to the barn. At night they roosted in the rafters, perched as closely together as they could snuggle, both for warmth and mutual protection. Charley would have no part of this social behavior. He would find his own perch, far from his dormitory mates. A favorite spot for the feisty rooster was the top of the sill of the lower window, permitting him a clear view outdoors so he could see the house. It was too cold a location for as frigid a night as we had just experienced.

"Charley was frozen right to the window pane, Dad," Bruce said. "He was frozen solid all along that side, from his shoulders to his thigh. He was still alive but I put him to sleep to save him any further pain."

There have been no more Charley Chickens at Twin Pines Farm.

9

On Getting Mechanized

The hard part of being a gentleman farmer came after the house was erected at Twin Pines Farm and we started thinking about a garden. The inventory of tools included hammer, handsaw, screwdrivers, pliers, and a measuring tape. Even I could see that something more was needed if we were to break through the solid sod of the area we planned for growing vegetables.

When I lived a few short years at Grandfather Barter's small farm in Avondale five decades ago, much of the work was done by hand. I was no stranger to spades, shovels, picks, digging bars, scythes, large wheel sandstones, stable fork, pitchfork, handsaws, crosscut saws, and axes, double-bitted and single-blade. So, at Twin Pines Farm, I made a list of implements I would need to transform part of a hay field into a Garden of Eden. Forget the crosscut saw, I thought, because I had a small chain saw that should handle any need of felling trees. Neither would I require hay or stable forks. What I did need was garden tools: pointed shovel, spade fork, rake and hoe. At that time I didn't even consider power tools, other than my trusty little chain saw.

It didn't take long to fill that short list and the sharp-tipped shovel, small pointed spade and digging fork looked as if they could handle any job, their working ends bright polished steel. Hoes and rakes were added for the finer work of weeding and raking the lawn-yard. It took only two minutes of digging to discover that I had forgotten a very important item: a pair of leather gloves. Painful blisters burst on my hands. I had outlined the area for the garden, using stakes and twine to mark the boundaries. When I placed the tip of the pointed shovel on the ground and used a foot to punch it into the soil it was like trying to dig pavement. That particular piece of ground hadn't seen a plough or harrow for many years.

It took days to clear even a small piece of ground, enough perhaps for a small herb garden. It was clear that thirty plus years in the newspaper business had softened the muscles, weakened the back and played tricks on my memory. There was nothing glamorous about this kind of work. It had no redeeming quality. I had never been called upon to break soil by hand in the past. I had used shovels, forks, rakes and hoes — but only with ground that had already been worked. Although Grandfather Sam had never owned a tractor in his life, he did have a horse, and a plough, a harrow and other moving machinery. If you're going to sow fields of oats, timothy, wheat, barley, flax or potatoes, you don't do it with a spading fork and shovel.

As I sat in the kitchen sipping a glass of tomato juice, rivulets of sweat streaking my hot face, I contemplated the blisters on my hands and did some serious cogitating. There must be an easier way to make a garden than this. There had to be. I had no desire to get a horse, even if there was an old horse-drawn hay rake on the property. Horses require a great deal of attention, need to be fed and watered regularly, require housing, expensive harness, and would not be used often enough to make it worthwhile or cost-effective. What I need is a tractor, I told myself, rationalizing that a tractor doesn't need to be fed, watered and housed. Right? Wrong!

I drove around the county observing tractors being used on farms, amazed at the number of different types available. They were all too big for what I required. Frankly, they scared the living daylights out of me; great, thundering, clanking machines, belching clouds of noxious fumes, pulling a gang plough that ripped into Mother Earth effortlessly, peeling back large brown slices of soil, or cutting and slicing at furrows with huge steel discs as the farmer harrowed a field. That would be a bit of overkill for me, I thought. I needed something smaller, big enough to plough and harrow a garden, but easier to handle — and less costly. There's no way I could afford one of the regular farm tractors, not even the smaller ones.

At that time garden tractors had just started making inroads among the earth-grubbing fraternity, more popular with lawn keepers because you could sit down and drive around while sharp blades scythed grass, dandelions and other weeds with equal ease. I looked around for something more than a riding mower and something less than a monster piece of machinery. It was a proud day when my 12 horsepower garden tractor was delivered to the farm, complete with the necessary implements: a single furrow plough, a small disc harrow, a snow blower, a steel dump cart and a three-bladed lawn mower. Here was a machine for all seasons, or so I thought.

For starters, it was a fun machine, a big toy for a man with a little boy's wonder of machinery; a tinkertoy that actually worked, with three forward gears and a reverse, one that could attain higher speeds than safety would permit except on the most level and straight runs. This is no toy, I had to remind myself sternly, this is a piece of machinery meant to till the soil, to create a garden. Still, I had some very enjoyable moments riding the tractor around the farm, up and down hill, getting used to the feel of it, becoming familiar with the gears, the steering, its hauling capabilities. It was not wasted time. I wasn't the only one enjoying the mighty mite. Bruce, Robert, Marshall and Doug all took turns having rides, and even Kay and Beth took turns at the wheel. Now it was time for some heavy work.

There was one major problem with that little tractor: it had no hydraulic system. When pulling the plough, the blade had to be lifted by brute strength, using a lever near your right side. This procedure had to be repeated quite often when ploughing a comparatively small garden. It was agony for the biceps, shoulder and back muscles when you reached back, grabbed the lever and tried to lift the plough clear of the ground so you could turn and start another furrow. It took some getting used to and the muscles slowly adapted to this new experience. The plough worked beautifully, slicing through the root-matted sod and turning over a roll of rich brown earth. I became too enthusiastic and ended up with a garden of about half an acre, a bit much for a household of two.

Then came the harrowing and that was something else again. The harrow that arrived with the tractor was of the disc variety, meant to cut the furrows and mix the soil to give the garden a fairly smooth surface. What our harrow did was bounce over the furrows and leave them practically unmarred. It was too light.

"That's what that rectangular frame is for, on top of the harrow," Robert advised. "You're supposed to add weights."

We did. Large field stones had a tendency to roll off as soon as the tractor started moving. Cement blocks were better at staying in place but the harrow still didn't do a very effective job on new furrows.

We decided that what we needed was a spring-tooth harrow, one that would rip those furrows apart. We found a section of a large harrow that had been given much use tearing up Carleton County soil. The section was about three feet square and we decided that would be just right for our mini-tractor. It was, though it also needed weights added to work properly. The combination of the spring-tooth harrow to break up the hard furrows, and the disc harrow to give a smooth surface soil was unbeatable. The mini-tractor had proven itself as a labor saver.

We found the tractor even more useful for moving materials about the farm, from earth and gravel to lumber and building supplies, not to mention its entertainment value as visiting young-sters were taken for rides. Soon we were driving down the steep hill to the river. This meant building a bridge across a gully half way down the hill, one that carried a mere trickle of water during the hot summers but was a raging flood during the spring runoff. Soon we were using the chain saw to fell some of the dead trees along the river front, cutting them up and splitting them in fireplace size. The tractor had no trouble at all pulling a fully loaded cart up the hill.

That little tractor became a part of the family, working without pay, demanding little in the way of food (fuel) and no water, asking only a minimum amount of maintenance. Even a klutz like me could operate this sturdy miniature beauty.

That is, even a klutz like me could operate the tractor and its implements during the summer and fall months. Winter proved more formidable. Twin Pines Farm has a very long driveway, forking at the top to give two entrances to Route 103. It is a gravel driveway, rough gravel from a nearby pit with a lot of sand and stones of varying sizes, from quarters to footballs. It is a challenging drive in the winter months once snow has arrived, and high, solid drifting is the rule rather than the exception. I looked forward to using the tractor's snow blower to keep a clear driveway.

I took a couple of swipes at the snow in the lower end of the driveway near the house, a level piece of ground with fine gravel. Son Bruce decided to tackle the driveway hill. You could see stones mixed in with the snow as the blower threw huge white plumes in the air and twenty or more feet to the side. Suddenly there was a loud bang, a grinding noise and the plume of snow stopped. So did the tractor. A large rock had caught in the propelling screw of the blower and put a brake on the operations. It was cleared and Bruce started again.

Not long after that there was a hideous shriek of protesting metal, harsh clanking and banging and all came to a halt again. The snow blower unit had been damaged beyond repair. Its final resting place is a spot near the barn and now wild raspberry bushes have circled the useless implement, shielding it from the scornful glances of its owner.

Unfortunately, the garden tractor is gone, too, the victim of an accident. If you haven't experienced the joy of living in Carleton County and working with its soil, you have no knowledge of our perennial battle with rocks. You can clear a field of the majority of the big rocks one year and the next spring they have been replaced. There are some really big ones, a challenge to be met only with a front-end loader. I was in Fredericton the day our tractor learned that it was not sturdy enough to withstand a major spill.

We had hired a man to help clear up the rocks around the yard, big ones that had appeared in the fill used around the cement foundation of the house. He used the tractor with its steel dump cart, picking up a load of stones and dumping them over the steep slope to the field below. Grandson Doug was an interested spectator from his viewpoint on the deck of the house. Doug was only five or six at the time but he knew the tractor, knew what to do and what not to do.

He was not at all impressed with the driving skill of the hired hand as the tractor was turned, the cart straightened and an attempt made to back it up to the edge of the ridge.

"Stop, stop!" Doug screamed, jumping up and down on the wooden deck and waving his hands. "You're going back too far, you'll go over!" he shouted, his face red with frustration as he tried to get the tractor driver's attention.

The hired hand either didn't hear the warning or ignored the young supervisor. Back and back the cart crept, closer and closer to the edge of the almost vertical drop of the bank, Doug continuing to scream his warning. Now the wheels of the cart were only inches from the edge, now at the very brink. The cart with its heavy load of rocks disappeared over the steep bank, dragging the tractor and its driver with it. The roar of the tractor engine, the bouncing of stones off steel, the shriek of tortured metal and breaking glass, and the intense shouting of young Doug brought Kay on the run.

At first she feared for the life of the hired hand. It was a miracle that he had survived the spill, hadn't been trapped by the cart of rocks or by the tractor. He climbed up the path nearby, seemingly none the worse for his harrowing experience, a sheepish, apologetic grin on his face.

"I told you, I told you!" Doug screamed. "I told you not to get so close!"

The tractor was a contorted mess, the hood torn off, lights broken, the steel tongue of the cart warped badly by the pull of a load of rocks in one direction and the tumbling tractor in another. The driver had managed to jump clear as the tractor and the heavily loaded cart plunged over the edge. It took a lot of manpower to disengage the cart from the tractor and to get the two twisted pieces of machinery back up over the bank to evaluate the seriousness of the damage.

We managed to repair the little tractor but it was never the same again. It lost more than its hood in the accident, it seemed to have lost its spirit. It survived for many years, being used less and less as a pulling beast, unable to gather the strength to pull a plough through tough soil, a mechanical invalid that spent its final days as a lawn mower at Robert and Beth's home, adjacent to Twin Pines Farm, with Marshall and Doug as attendants. It was an ignoble end for this once spunky little labor saver.

We've had one other tractor at Twin Pines Farm, one of the big ones. Kay and I had moved out to Regina for a year where I worked for the *Leader Post*, one of the nation's fine daily newspapers. A major reason for the move was to be a lot closer to son Ian and his growing family. They lived in Brooks, Alberta, a day's drive from Regina and we were able to visit Ian, his wife Susan, and children Erin and Jessa (a third daughter, Haley, has been added since then) fairly often during our stay out west. When we were returning to Twin Pines Farm to live, David Henley, owner and publisher of that fine community newspaper, *The Bugle*, asked me to join his staff as editorial director. During the negotiations I jokingly suggested that a tractor for the farm was one of my conditions of acceptance. Time went by and no more was thought of the matter. Though the little tractor had become nothing more than a riding lawn mower, we had been introduced to the mechanized tiller.

If you want to develop sore shoulders in a hurry, get yourselves one of those rototillers that are propelled forward only by the action of the tines turning in the soil. The tines are in front of the unmotorized wheels. It is unrefined torture as the beast snorts and roars, bouncing wildly when rocks are encountered, straining to wrench the handles from your grasp, stretching muscles you never knew you had. The garden no longer had to be ploughed and harrowed each year as the soil was well worked. A tiller would do the trick, I thought. It will — but don't settle for one of those shoulder-jarring monsters. A tiller with motorized wheels and front-end drive is well worth the money.

We managed to get along with the torture machine for some time, the thought of another tractor never being considered. Then came the day when I arrived home at supper hour and found a gleaming red tractor parked in the driveway in front of the garage, the steering column festooned with a huge ribboned bow. Who is parking their tractor in my driveway, I wondered, and why the decorations? I lost no time in climbing up the side and sitting on the steel seat, gripping the steering wheel. An envelope was attached to the black rim and the card it contained told the story: From David and Marlene. I sat there for some time, stunned by this sudden change in circumstances, my mind racing with plans for the future.

The Henleys had not forgotten that I had asked for a tractor. This old fellah had obviously seen a lot of service over Carleton County fields but it had been rebuilt and given fresh red paint from stem to stern. It was one of the happiest moments in my life, one I'll never forget. The tractor was a big sucker! Though overjoyed at having my own tractor, I admit to being a bit scared when I looked down from my lofty perch; it seemed a long way to the ground. Supper was delayed that night as I moved the tractor back and forth, getting used to the gears, the brakes, and the idea that this was a big toy for a big boy.

Now that I had a "real" tractor, I wasn't sure what I was going to do with it. I had never before climbed aboard such a large one, obviously hadn't driven one, and wasn't at all sure what I could use it for. I had no attachments: no plough, no harrow, no wagon. It did have a front-end loader and I had fun raising and lowering the bucket. That could be used for snow removal, I thought. For quite some time I used it as my private vehicle to tour the upper reaches of Twin Pines Farm. I was too chicken (and probably wise) to take it down the steep hill of the property, or to drive it across the side of slopes. Winter came and I quickly discovered that the tractor was practically useless on our steep driveway. It needed a set of chains at the very least, as well as a lot of additional weight in the rear as the front-end loader at the front resulted in little traction for the big tires.

The loader could certainly lift and get rid of huge bites of snow, but that was of little use if you couldn't get the tractor wheels to grip the snow and ice enough to move. Son Bruce is no stranger to machines but even he couldn't clear our steep driveway of snow. Over the winter months I thought of what use I could make of the tractor come spring. It had hydraulic power to the front-end loader but not to the rear, though the power take-off unit operated perfectly. George Pepper, a frequent visitor at Twin Pines Farm before he moved to the United States, suggested that I attend a used tractor and equipment auction and get a gang plough. He assured me that he could hook up the hydraulics.

It was an exciting spring day when George and I got up early and headed out to a sale of used farm machinery. A field was filled with tractors, ploughs, harrows, binders, seeders, sprayers and other machinery. It was my first trip to such an event and I was overwhelmed by the variety of equipment available. We finally settled on a three-furrow plough. George promised me that my tractor would be able to pull the blue monster with no problem. Perhaps so. I was more concerned about my own ability to handle the combination of tractor and monstrous plough. When hitched together they would make a long train and it seemed to me that it would be difficult to make turns, even though I had witnessed many farmers handling even larger tractors and gang ploughs with ridiculous ease.

Once the plough was delivered to Twin Pines Farm, George spent countless hours repairing the hydraulics, replacing parts that had been removed for one reason or another, hooking up pipes and tubing, testing and re-testing. Finally he announced that the job was done. It was a formidable sight: the large red tractor hooked up to the much longer blue plough. It was also intimidating. Not to worry, George assured me. He climbed onto the tractor seat, started the motor, put it into gear and started forward, leaving three perfect furrows of brown earth. It would have been great if I planned to plough the large fields on the farm, to sow grain crops or plant acres of potatoes. It proved impractical for our garden, the space being too small to use the big plough. By the time the tractor reached the end of a row the plough would have finished only part of the route. The way we had laid out the garden, with barn and henyard in the way at one end and the yard-lawn at the other, there simply wasn't enough room to manoeuvre the plough. It and the tractor sat unused at the farm for a year or more and finally they were sold. The fault rested not with the tractor or plough but with me.

The old shoulder-wrenching tiller was disposed of too, and we purchased a larger one with motorized wheels in front and motorized tines in back. It was easy to use, did a tremendous job of tilling the soil, and caused no unnecessary aches and pains. The best part of it was that Kay could use it as well as I could, it being a user-friendly piece of equipment

You could steer this orange beast with one hand and it seldom gave any trouble. Kay's expertise in maintenance, honed over the years as she took care of a succession of power lawn mowers, kept the tiller going for years. Just recently the size of the garden shrank as we developed the use of raised beds for our vegetables and herbs. There was no need for such a large tiller. It was traded in for a less powerful unit, one even more easily handled, small enough to turn the soil in the raised beds.

10

A Greenhouse Fiasco

Robert and I have one obsession in common: we always try to rush spring, to get plants started while the snow is still deep on the ground and temperatures well below freezing. Each year, much to the despair of Kay and Beth, we have flats and pots taking up valuable space in living rooms, dining rooms and anywhere else they can receive light and steady heat. It's an obsession shared by thousands across this great land and one that appears earlier each year. We have the seed catalogue houses to thank for this, I suppose. It used to be that new catalogues appeared in late winter, in plenty of time for ordering seed for the coming spring. Now the catalogues appear in our mail boxes before Christmas.

Our mutual love of early planting led to the magnificent fiasco of the Twin Pines Farm greenhouse, an example of country carpentry that resulted in a costly renovation to the house in later years. It all started when I had the bright idea of taking advantage of the deck that ran the full length of the house on the east side. It seemed a brilliant idea at the time, maximizing space already provided, but there was a flaw in our thinking.

In the first place, when the deck was designed by the builder he made an error in judgment. The boards of the deck were nailed close together with no allowance for rain to drain through, and the slope allowed was not sufficient to permit rain or melted snow to drain off properly. It was not a tongue-and-groove floor but it was fairly watertight, a fact that I welcomed, in my ignorance, as the space under it seemed like an ideal place to stack fireplace wood and keep it dry. It served that purpose admirably. It also sparked the idea of closing in an area underneath the deck for a greenhouse. Robert looked over the situation and agreed that it could be done and wouldn't require a great deal of work.

He was right. When we had the house built we made sure there were plenty of electrical outlets, both inside and outside, for the convenience of power appliances and tools. There are two such outlets on the east side of the house for use on the deck, and two on the first story, underneath the deck. This made the job of building a greenhouse an easy task when it came to sawing two-by-fours for studs and boards for walls. Again we used rough hemlock for our construction, feeling that it would be ideal material for a greenhouse, realizing there would be perpetual dampness. Actually it was more a job of framing than creating a building, as most of the structure would be glass — except for the wall of the house that would make one side, and the solid roof of the deck above.

We wanted a glass greenhouse not one of plastic. Fortunately, Robert and Beth had a generous supply of storm windows that he had saved after renovations to their 13-room home in Woodstock, where aluminum replaced wood. These were of varying widths but all of the same length. He had more than sufficient to complete the greenhouse. We closed in the east side of the structure level with the outside of the deck. This permitted the light and heat of the sun to penetrate from the time it rose over the hill directly opposite our house. We then built a six-foot extension of the greenhouse to the south so there would be glass east, west and south, with a sloping glass roof. It worked out just the way we planned it. We boarded in the north side, built and installed a door, and devised a way to get those seeds into the ground weeks, if not months, earlier than waiting for the garden to thaw and the soil to warm.

It was a comfortable little greenhouse, about eight feet wide and fifteen long. The floor was earth, a feature we felt would allow for more humidity. Hemlock boards were used to make a long work table, large enough that we both could use it while adding soil to pots and flats, planting seeds, watering, and the many other chores. It was kind of a crazy quilt of a structure with its glass surfaces broken frequently by the framing of the windows and the structures we added to hold them in place. Many of the windows had ventilations flaps that could be opened to admit outside air.

A Greenhouse Fiasco

Early the next year Robert and I enjoyed ourselves as we leafed through seed catalogues, filled out orders, and prepared for our first efforts at gardening under glass. We had the foresight to fill a wooden potato barrel with earth the previous fall to mix with peat moss and vermiculite to make our own potting soil. We were ready to go, with visions of fresh tomatoes, cucumbers, peppers and other vegetables thrusting their green tips through the good planting mixture we had created. We soon discovered that, though we were ready to go, Mother Nature had other ideas. She sets the limits of light and heat units, the length of days, the heat of day and cold of night. The greenhouse would heat up miraculously during sunny days in February even when temperatures outside were below freezing. At night the mercury would drop dramatically, both outdoors and in the greenhouse. Something had to be done to give more control over widely fluctuating temperatures.

No provision had been made to heat the greenhouse. We had thought only of the heat of the sun. There are ways of capturing and storing a lot of that heat by the use of containers full of water, and other means, a passive heat that would control to some degree the temperature of the greenhouse at night. We hadn't included any such plans. Our answer was electric heat since we had a power outlet at our disposal within the structure and no flue for a stove.

The planting went ahead in flats and pots on the work table, thrust into the south end so as to capture as much heat and light as possible. At night the table was covered with a large sheet of clear heavy plastic, an electric heater with a thermostat placed beneath the table, giving bottom heat to the flats and pots, but also supplying heat to the top as the warm air circulated up the sides of the plastic. This jerrybuilt heating system worked. It was not cost effective! Our electric power bill zoomed. We were probably growing our vegetables at a cost of two dollars per tomato or cucumber. The reward was the satisfaction of having green, growing plants while the snow remained deep outside and temperatures still frigid. We were a step ahead of most New Brunswick gardeners.

I'm an experimenter. I like to try vegetables and fruit not commonly grown in Carleton County's temperature zone. Peanuts started in the greenhouse and transplanted to the garden were a wonder to the eye and a great conversational gambit when visitors came. Peanut plants have a spectacular rich yellow flower. However, even with a head start in the greenhouse, New Brunswick is not the ideal place to grow this crop. There are not enough heat units in our short season. Though small peanut tubers did develop under our plants, they didn't have sufficient time to reach maturity. We've had better luck with watermelons some years, but they are iffy and most gardeners can't be bothered trying them.

The greenhouse did prove a success in many ways, despite the obvious fact that the cost of heating made it impractical to get too early a start. That first year we did have fresh tomatoes and cucumbers to eat weeks before they were ready in other area gardens. Some plants were kept in the greenhouse and the product went from there straight to the dining table. Heat became another serious problem in the summer months as the mercury inside climbed to incredible highs. The flaps on the windows, the panels that opened, could not start to provide the cooling ventilation necessary. Nor did propping the door wide open.

We decided against installing electric fans or making other changes to achieve better control of summer temperatures. Instead, we decided not to start our spring planting so early, thus avoiding the necessity of using electric heat to save plants from freezing at nights. The solution to high temperatures during the summer was to transplant everything, to keep no crops inside. Finally, after several years, we decided that the greenhouse was not practical and had caused more problems than it solved. Window panes broke all too frequently, exposed as they were to dramatic changes in temperatures and to flying rocks and other missiles. We got tired of buying glass for these large windows and chose hard plastic — and this didn't work too well. Maintenance included replacing glass and putty, cleaning windows, painting and staining wood, storing an ever growing accumulation of wooden flats, pots, greenhouse string and tools.

A Greenhouse Fiasco

There was an even better reason for abandoning our greenhouse experiment and tearing it down. It was destroying our house! We became aware of this major problem when some of the boards in the deck (the roof of the greenhouse) became springy, soft when walked upon. They were rotting. So was the framing around the double windows in the library-den-office which shared a common wall with the greenhouse. In fact, that had been one of the pleasures enjoyed. The office windows could be swung wide open allowing the primeval scent of damp earth and growing plants to pervade the den. This was a luxury when it was still freezing outside, fields covered with snow. It proved to be an expensive luxury. Rot had invaded other areas of the house, between the deck and the east wall. We were in trouble.

It was a sad day when we tore down the greenhouse. It had been a good structure, though odd-appearing. We'd even taken the time and material to shingle the exterior and give it an attractive stain. Even more rot was discovered as we demolished the greenhouse, pieces of window frames breaking off in our hands as we separated them from the studs. Heat, humidity and insufficient ventilation had combined to allow the penetration of deadly rot. A thorough inspection of the deck floor, the east side of the house where the greenhouse had been built, and the double windows in the den confirmed our worst fears.

It was obvious that professional help was needed. A Hartland contractor was asked to come and inspect the house and recommend what had to be done. The diagnosis was sobering: building a totally new deck, tearing open the side of the house to discover the extent of rot, removing the double windows in the office and installing a new frame to hold them. We decided to go even further, since a good part of the east side had to be opened anyway; we would remove all siding from the east side and apply insulation board to save on energy costs. The builder agreed that this would be a good idea (eventually we would do the same to all sides of the house and the added insulation has made winters more comfortable inside).

The builder and his crew did a great job of renovating and

repairing the house. He explained that outside decks can and do cause problems when not properly installed. He suggested the use of preservative-treated wood for the uprights, rails and flooring. The boards should be spaced to allow rain and melting snow to drip through to the ground below, thus creating no opportunities for water to gather and encourage pockets of rot. It was amazing just how much rot was discovered when the reconstruction took place. It was a wonder the den windows hadn't fallen free of their rot-infested frames, that no one had put a foot through the weakened deck. We've had no problems with the deck or the east side of the house since that time, nor have we built a second greenhouse attached to the house.

That doesn't mean that Robert and I have given up our annual drive to start planting early. Once again the living and dining rooms have been pressed into service, mini-greenhouses incorporated into our planning, pots and potting soil used to get those seeds germinating before their usual time. We're always looking for new varieties of seeds, new gimmicky containers, tools and growing aids. It doesn't seem to matter if our experiments are successful or not. The urge to get fingers and hands in soil, to plant seeds, to experience that sense of wonder when tender green shoots push through the earth, comes like clockwork each year, perhaps a bit earlier in our homes than in most.

I've learned a great deal about greenhouses since our little fiasco, have visited many and written a number of articles on the subject. I've also learned that the professionals don't use the common garden variety of seeds and that most of them start with seedlings grown in other greenhouses.

Ben Baldwin of Douglasfield, near Chatham, is one of the province's entrepreneurial greenhouse market gardeners. He and his wife, Wera, operate two greenhouses on their Century farm in a small Miramichi community, as well as planting many acres of vegetables, fruit and grain. Their products are much in demand at the farm market in Newcastle each week and they do a good business at their farm gate.

A Greenhouse Fiasco

Ben introduced me to the delights of greenhouse tomatoes and cucumbers, as well as lettuce grown under plastic. Kay and I happened by the Baldwin farm one day when he had just completed planting his vegetable seedlings, their green stems thrusting up through slits in black plastic. When we were leaving for our return trip to Wakefield, I was given a number of tomato and cucumber seedlings that had been left over from the planting. I was too polite to decline the kind offer but wondered what I would do with the plants. I no longer had a greenhouse and it was still winter weather; the garden wouldn't be ready for planting for two months at the earliest.

The bay window of our living room became our greenhouse, other plants relocated to make room for pots of tomato and cucumber plants. What Ben hadn't told me was that the varieties he had given me were climbers, not sprawlers. As weeks went by I had to affix cords from the drapery rod to the plants as the tomatoes and cucumbers grew and grew. They kept climbing and eventually reached the drapery rod. They were removed from their bench and the pots placed on the floor, and still they grew, up and up. Eventually the plants were seven feet tall and it still wasn't time to transplant them to the garden. The tomatoes and cucumbers received plenty of light from the window and the foliage became so dense that it darkened the room. We had tomatoes from those house grown plants before they were transplanted, and after. The cucumbers didn't take kindly to transplanting but they too eventually gave us a crop.

11
Genesis of a Pond

The pond snuggles into the hill side below the lower lawn, a jewel fighting a losing battle against time and nature. Experts advised me that it couldn't be done, that you don't create a pond on the slope of a hill, especially so when the hill is nothing more than a huge gravel bed. Nevertheless, the pond was created and it has given much pleasure to the residents of and visitors to Twin Pines Farm. I was determined to have a pond, both for cosmetic value and spiritual enrichment. It has been a joy!

The water source for the pond is a trickle-stream from the spring dug in the side of the hill about fifty feet to the northwest, our first source of drinking water at the farm. This small brook is fed by other underground veins of water as it gurgles toward the pond. A bulldozer carved a deep cut into the side of the hill, the earth moved, forming the lower and southern banks of the pond. It was immediately apparent that the experiment would be a failure without immediate help. Gravel is not a retainer of water. Clay would make a good liner but none was available on the farm, nor did we know of any nearby source that could be tapped.

Heavy plastic was an option and we decided to give it a try; it would certainly be easier to put into position than attempting to line the pond with clay. Easier yes, but easy — no! Grounds crews at major league baseball parks make it look easy when they unroll huge tarps to cover the infield and protect it from the rain. Handling large rolls of heavy plastic and trying to get it to fit into a pond is something else again, an exhausting challenge. There were cheers when the plastic was finally in place, the stream from the spring diverted, and water started to trickle into the pond. The next morning we were amazed to find the pond filled and overflowing. It didn't take long to dig a shallow overflow drain, thus assuring that the pond would always have fresh water, at the same time lessening the possibility of pressure bursting the lower (and weaker) bank.

The small spring uphill was the genesis of this strange little pond but the changes that have occurred since then have been awe-inspiring. When it was first created it was surrounded by bulldozer-scarred earth and gravel with a multitude of famous Carleton County stones, some very large. The exception was the north end of the pond where the stream trickled through a small clump of weed trees, a source of pussy willows each spring. We soon learned that when you start a pond you unleash the powers of nature to create life, plant and animal. Each day brings something new to the small aquatic miracle.

You have to pay frequent visits to the pond to see the many changes. When first created, a water-mirror in a desert of gravel, it was a marvel to the eye and easily observed from a chair on the deck of the house. The first visitors were birds, flying in for a drink or a bath, swallows swooping low over the water to snatch a meal in flight. Then aquatic insects took up residence in the pond, masses of jellied frog eggs floated on the surface, sprigs of green growth pushed gravel aside and colored the banks. The scene changed before our very eyes. Bird droppings sowed seeds in and around the pond and the scarred gravel took on a coat of brown and green.

The changes were not confined to the perimeter of the pond; the water teemed with life. Tadpoles appeared as if by magic. I wanted to give nature a hand, to introduce fish. I visited a nearby hatchery with the intention of purchasing some brook trout. I was told that this was impossible, that the trout were raised for introduction to rivers, streams and lakes in the province. Some were sold to land owners but only in quantities in the hundreds or thousands. I replied that I didn't have a lake or a big pond, that I wanted only a few to see whether they could be raised in such a small body of water. The result was a gift of twenty brookies, each about five inches long. They were taken home and dumped into the crystal clear water. Would they survive in a pond that was only three feet at its deepest point?

Was there sufficient food to keep the trout alive? I decided that I would not feed the fish, a true test of the ability of the pond to supply and attract food. There were exceptions to this rule; we soon discovered that the trout loved to eat raw hamburger and/or ground steak. We were delighted when the speckled fish would swim to the edge of the pond and take the ground meat from our fingers. It became a ritual for us to hand-feed the trout as well as conversation piece for visitors to the farm, all of whom asked if they could feed the fish. This also resulted in numerous cut fingers as trout zoomed in to snatch a piece of meat, sharp teeth often drawing blood.

There was no feeding of the fish with commercial food as is done in hatcheries and in some private ponds. The trout seemed to thrive on the food supplied by nature, both that in the water and the unfortunate insects that landed on the surface. The spring provided a steady source of fresh, pure water, cold enough that the pond did not become dangerously warm for the trout even on the hottest summer day. Our fears that the spring would dry up during a drought seemed to be unfounded. Silt was a problem for both the spring and the pond. It wasn't too hard a job to dig out the spring; it has been much more difficult to control silt in the pond. The big question that first year of the trout was: can they survive the winter?

It was a question we worried about for many months as a transparent hard skin of ice covered the surface of the water, becoming more translucent as the ice thickened. Soon the surface was covered with snow, the trout lost from view. The spring brook never gave up its job of supplying fresh water to the pond, even when temperatures dropped twenty or more degrees below freezing. All winter long there was open water at the north end of the pond where, sheltered by willows from the prevailing wind, the stream supplied a continuous flow. Finally spring arrived, the snow melted, and the ice became thinner each day, appearing to be black now that its mantle of white had disappeared.

Then one day the ice was gone and we made an anxious trip to the pond to see whether any of the trout had survived. The speckled beauties were there, darting around the pond in search of food. They welcomed a ration of ground meat and had evidently retained their memory of hand feeding for they lost no time in coming close to the shore, mouths gaping like fledglings in a nest waiting for the return of mother bird. We took a head count and discovered that our school of speckled trout had lost a few members over the winter. There were no bodies floating in the pond and we assumed that the cannibalistic trout had feasted on a few of their weaker brothers and sisters. Still, the experiment had been a success; the pond could maintain fish. It remained to be seen how long they would continue to survive.

Our trout survived three winters, with a few losses, but we still had a dozen and now they were bigger, ten or eleven inches in length. It was a spiritual experience to sit on the bank of the pond, reflecting on the changes that had taken place, and watching the multi-hued, speckled fish swimming lazily or darting furiously as they hunted for food. The transformation of the pond and its immediate area was amazing over a few short years. Beautiful sumacs now covered the eastern bank, having claimed the territory from wild raspberry canes. Grass grew to the water line and several willows took root. The pond itself, getting shallower each year as silt built up, was invaded by aquatic plants, including bulrushes. A lone poplar pushed through the gravel on the southwest corner and now stands fifteen feet.

A precursor of the ultimate fate of the trout appeared one spring morning with the arrival of a blue heron at the pond. The water was deep, swollen by runoff from the hill above, and the heron, despite its very long legs, was unable to spear any of the speckled dinner treats. Apparently herons have as long a memory as elephants, for a blue heron appeared again in late summer. It was a dry year and the level of the water was the lowest it had been since the pond was built. We noted the visitor as we sat at the table eating breakfast and watched through the picture window. He was still there, standing and staring as we left for town. When we checked the pond in late afternoon, all of the trout were gone!

We have never restocked the pond with trout, or with any other fish. It is no longer deep enough after years of silting. However, it remains a major attraction at Twin Pines Farm and serves a useful purpose, a watering hole for animals and birds, a haven for aquatic insects and frogs, a garden for aquatic plants, a constant source of education for the observant onlooker.

One of the rituals of spring each year is the "explosion of frogs," an event that must be seen to be believed. It seems that frogs burrow deep into the silt at the bottom of the pond to survive the winter. After the ice has melted in the spring, when the water temperature is just right and, perhaps, the sun sends some secret message, the frogs abandon their silt homes and explode to the surface. Kay was the first to notice this spectacular sight.

"Come and look, Jim," she shouted, as she stood on the deck by the glass patio doors, "the water in the pond seems to be boiling."

And so it was. Circular ripples spread as the surface of the pond was broken in dozens of different places. You could hear the sound, almost a wet popping, as more and more "holes" appeared in the water. I grabbed the ever-handy binoculars and handed them to Kay. "They're frogs!" she said, handing me the field glasses. That's what they were.

We walked down to the pond and could see hundreds of frogs swimming around in the water, looking almost like people doing the breast stroke, as their long back legs powered in perfect harmony. A swimming frog is a sight to behold but an "explosion of frogs" is a dramatic sight seldom seen. You have to be at the right place at the precise time to witness this spectacular display by nature. There are no instant replays. We watch for this phenomenon every spring and because we are at home most of the time we're usually fortunate enough to see it.

There's a lot to be seen by nature watchers at Twin Pines Farm (or any farm) if eyes are kept open. We've spotted moose standing in the pond eating aquatic plants, a deer having a drink, visiting ducks dropping in for a rest before heading north or south, a resident fox using the pond both as a watering hole and as a stalking ground. There's action during each season, colors change as trees dress themselves in green in the spring and are transformed in the fall, the sumacs a rich red. All of the senses come into play as the pond evolves in nature.

Genesis of a Pond

So, I thought, if one pond produces such incredible changes, surely two would be even better. If I could develop a second one and make it deeper, perhaps we could get back to raising trout. I contacted a contractor who had the necessary heavy equipment to build another pond, talked it over with him, and decided to go ahead.

It was a disaster looking for a place to happen — and it did. Perhaps it could have been avoided if only I had been home the day the men and equipment arrived. I had several options in mind: to build a second pond to the north of the present one at the site of the spring, the overflow to feed the original pond; or a pond to be excavated to the west at the site of the original farm well, the overflow to feed the first pond; or to dig a second pond south of the first one and fed by its overflow.

I arrived home to find that the third option had been adopted. The earth moving equipment had hit heavy shale and it was decided to move earth and gravel from the side hill to build a pond. A furrow was scored from the old well down hill to the new pond and plastic pipe buried to feed it water. It was also fed by overflow from the original pond. This was an expensive mistake. The second pond remains, a monument to my own stupidity. When you build a pond with gravel sides and bottom, you've built a large sieve. The only time the second pond is ever filled is in the spring when the ground is still frozen and there's a heavy runoff of melting snow, combined with the snow in the pond itself. Adding insult to injury, there's now a steep and dangerous bank where the side of the hill was torn off to create the second pond. This makes it impossible to drive a tractor over this particular spot. The slope became a steep bank.

We tried hard to salvage something from the fiasco, using a plastic liner in the pond but we ran out of plastic before the job was completed and decided it was just too much of a hassle. Pond number two is nothing but a circular hole with grass and weeds hiding the earth-brown scar of man's folly. Winter adds a white blanket to keep the error out of sight.

The grand experiment is not over. The saga is not complete.

12

Fancy Feathers

Most people in rural areas raise poultry for two reasons: eggs and meat. That's the practical approach but, as already explained, our Charley Chickens, I and II, were pets. There came a time when we wanted the more practical approach to poultry farming but even then we wanted to be different. So do thousands of other feather-fanciers and this is one of the reasons that Bantams play a major role in poultry farming — for eggs, meat and for show birds.

Our first step in building a flock was to find a source of supply for these non-standard breeds. We always had a number of magazines and papers in the house dealing with the interests of small farms and "back to the land" types. I became very interested in the hens that lay blue or green eggs, the Araucanas which originated in the mountains of Chile. A Canadian poultry paper listed breeders across the nation who supplied exotic poultry breeds but named no Araucana breeder in New Brunswick. Where could I find them?

Poultry farmers have their own communication grapevine and it wasn't too long before we had obtained the name of a breeder at Turtle Creek, near Moncton, who raised and sold Araucanas.

It's a long drive from Wakefield to the Moncton area to pick up a few chickens, nearly 200 miles, but Bruce and I were determined and we made the trip. We found our man and our chickens and returned home in high spirits. We were ready to start our own breeding program.

Araucanas come in two varieties, rumpless and tailed, when bred in the pure strain. Standard colors for show purposes are black, dark brown, silver and white. I don't believe any of our Araucanas ever met these strict standards. Our birds were more colorful, with reddish brown, gold or bronze feathers mixing with black, silver and white. The roosters had magnificent tails and colorful ruffs. One of the eggs produced by this small flock was hatched in Bruce's homemade incubator and became Charley Chicken II.

At that time there was a great controversy about Araucana eggs, some breeders claiming that they were a health food because they contained less cholesterol than those from standard breeds, such as New Hampshire Reds and White Leghorns. The majority of scientific studies I have read pooh-pooh such extravagant claims. There is apparently little difference between the health giving properties of hens' eggs.

There is a parallel controversy over the benefits of white or brown-shelled eggs. White eggs, usually from White Leghorns, have thinner shells than browns, usually from New Hampshire Reds or other breeds. Araucana eggs are smaller than those of their larger cousins and have a shell that is thicker than that of a white egg. After thousands of cooking and taste tests, residents of and visitors to Twin Pines Farm have decided that there's not much if any difference between any of these eggs. Any difference in quality and flavor comes in the age of the egg, not the breed of the hen.

It didn't take long for our Araucana eggs to reach consumers. We found a ready market for them, both because of their blue shell and the fact that they sized out as mediums, neither too large nor too small. The flock continued to build and so did our list of customers for these colorful eggs. Many wanted to visit the farm to see the hens for themselves, perhaps not believing our biased praise of their beauty. They left impressed, exclaiming over the rich colors of the hens and the stately bearing of the proud roosters. We decided to experiment with Bantams even more, to introduce other breeds.

Not all exotic breeds of poultry are Bantams, nor are all Bantams necessarily small. When we decided to expand our flock to include varieties other than Araucanas we studied a long list of possibilities: feather-legged; rose-comb clean-legged; single-comb clean-legged; all other combed clean-legged. There were numerous breeds within these categories.

Once again we were limited in choice by what was available

within a reasonable distance of Twin Pines Farm. We ended up with Cochins and Silkies from the feather-legged group and Houdans from the "all other" combed clean-legged breeds (to which Araucanas also belong).

The Cochin is the most popular of the feathered leg Bantam. It appeared in England in 1860, not bred down from the large Cochin but brought back from China by soldiers who had served there. The original foundation birds were buff but because of crossbreeding Cochin Bantams now come in a variety of colors, including buff, black and white. Experts say there is no better breed of Bantam birds for those with limited or confined space. Silkies, on the other hand, are one of the most attractive Bantam varieties. They get their name from the down or hairlike texture of their plumage. A unique feature is the dark violet color of their skin. White Silkies are the most numerous but they also come in golden, black, blue and partridge colors. There are both bearded and non-bearded varieties.

Houdans, developed in France, come in white, black and mottled colors. It is easy to get mottled birds by crossing a black and a white. This lively little bird was one of my favorites. They were impossible to keep in the high-fenced henyard without resorting to roofing the pen with chicken wire. The Houdans would fly to the top of the barn, then take off and soar several hundred feet to the large pine near the house.

One of our Houdan hens caused us great concern one day when she disappeared. Knowing her propensity to escape confinement we didn't worry, at first. We were sure she would return home by lights out. She didn't. Then we did worry. Three weeks later she appeared, strutting from the woods to the south, up through the meadow to the chicken yard — followed by a hatch of tiny, fluffy chickens. Judging by the colors of the chicks after they developed their feathers, Charley Chicken II and Mrs. Houdan had engaged in an affair.

The addition of these new Bantams to our flock resulted in quite a few intermarriages, and a change in the size and colorings of our hens and roosters. Bantams are the best of all breeds when it comes to hatching eggs nature's style, under a hen.

These small hens are wonderful mothers once the chicks have arrived but, more importantly, they are faithful brooders, patiently nestling on their clutch of eggs day after day, rising to turn the eggs when instinct prompts them to do so, aggressively rebuffing any interlopers.

Now that we had a curious mix of laying hens, a wide variety of colors, shapes and sizes, we decided that we should obtain some meat poultry, those ungainly birds raised for no other reason than to provide meat for the table. By this time we had two freezers going, one for vegetables and fruit, the other for meat products.

We had never raised this type of poultry and our Bantam hens and roosters were really not the answer to roaster or broiling chickens, being too small. The decision to raise Meat Kings, one of the most popular of this variety of poultry, also meant finding housing as they couldn't be kept with our other fowl. There was a sturdy building just below the terrace of the lawn that had been used by Bruce to raise a pig. Now it became a town house for Meat Kings.

There had been a pole fence around the house to give Mrs. Pig an exercise yard. We extended this with chicken wire to accommodate our flock of Meat Kings. When they arrived as chicks they didn't seem much different than White Leghorns but it didn't take long to see that these white birds were a special breed.

Meat Kings were developed to produce a hen, rooster or capon with outsized breasts, meaning more white meat. Most of these birds raised by commercial growers are "harvested" when they reach the size to be sold as broilers. There's a reason for this, as we discovered. Poultry developed to be used for their meat are gluttons; they eat and drink, eat and drink. As they become heavier they become more ungainly and some find it difficult to move around well. It is not unusual for these birds to have problems with their hips and legs. They are, collectively, the "couch potato" of the poultry world, much averse to exercise but fond of food and drink.

It was while we had the Meat Kings that an incident occurred that was and remains a mystery. Each night the Meat Kings were put in their house and the door closed tight, knowing that we have a res-

resident fox family at Twin Pines Farm, as well as other predators with a taste for chicken. One morning we went down to feed the Meat Kings and discovered that one was missing. There had seemingly been an explosion of white feathers in the house. The only clue we had was a knothole in one of the hemlock boards on the lower side. There was blood around the hole, both inside and out, as well as a profusion of white feathers. It was almost as if a hen had stuck her head out the knothole, been grabbed by some animal and pulled through. That was impossible. The hen was too large and the hole too small for such an action.

Did a weasel or mink get into the hen house, slice up a chicken and pass it piece by piece through the knothole to a waiting partner? Nature provides many mysteries and we are not always able to explain them. This was so in the case of the missing Meat King. Many theories were offered but no logical explanation was ever accepted. It could have been a prank by some practical joker who stole a chicken and at the same time baffled us with false clues, such as blood running down the boards on the inside and outside from a knothole, scattered white feathers confusing the issue even more. We like to think it was something more mysterious, more sinister, part of Twin Pines Farm's folklore.

The Meat Kings experiment was a success, at least a partial one. We did "harvest" the birds, did have a steady supply of our own chickens over the winter. It is doubtful if it was cost effective: by the time you purchased the chicks, bought the feed (and they are great eaters), carried water to them, captured escapees, lost some to health problems (or mysterious disappearances), they probably cost more per pound than you would pay at the supermarket.

Actually, that's a cop-out. The truth is that Kay and I didn't enjoy the "harvesting" process. I was the man with the axe, the designated executioner. I do not enjoy the taking of life, whether it be an animal, our feathered friends of the wild, or even a "stupid" chicken. It's a messy job at best. I abhor it.

Kay has the same attitude about plucking birds of their feathers, cleaning and dressing them, an odorous task that involves too many of the senses. There is no smell equal to that experienced when a feathered chicken is plunged into a pot of boiling water to make plucking an easier chore. This is particularly true when you have a production line going, not one but many birds. It was a long time after our first day of "harvesting" before chicken was served at our table. That was the end of the Meat Kings project!

We had one more adventure in the raising of hens but this time we did it the easy way: we purchased a flock of New Hampshire Reds from a farm that specializes in egg producers. The Reds are famous for their brown eggs and the ones we obtained had gone through a full laying season. They were a valuable addition to our henyard because they were still good producers and they were large enough to be used for meat purposes once their laying days were over. This mixture of Bantams and Reds produced some interesting looking chicks the next year, unusual combinations of color and sizes.

Our adventure in raising ducks gave much more pleasure, as well as tragedy. We figured that since we had a pond, partly as a cosmetic highlight at the farm, why not make it an even more beautiful sight by having ducks swimming around? We were used to having wild ducks drop in for a short visit from time to time, usually in the spring, and they added a nice dimension to the pond. We purchased a drake and two mother ducks from Stephen Porter. Stephen is to ducks what poultry-expert Bernard Phillips of Upper Woodstock is to exotic poultry. Stephen has raised all kinds of poultry at his Houlton Road farm but specializes in ducks, many of which have awed residents and tourists alike as they cavort in and around the spectacularly beautiful pond at the famous Karnes Bakery plant in Woodstock, an attraction for area residents and for tourists.

Bernie specializes in exotic birds and has won many awards at shows across the Maritimes. A visit to either spread is a delight for feather-fanciers, those of us who look for something more exciting than traditional birds can offer. We search for character!

The ducks from Stephen's farm had no problem at all adapting to life at Twin Pines where the pond offered them new adventures. We also felt they enjoyed being a threesome, no longer having to compete with a flock of other birds for a kernel of corn. It was with a sense of anticipation that we moved a small dog house to the lower bank of the pond, a few steps from the water, hoping that the mother ducks would take the hint and make it a home. One tried. She laid several eggs in a nest she built on the floor of her home. Then one night some predator raided the nest and feasted on the eggs. She would have nothing more to do with the dog house.

Mrs. Duck's mothering instinct was still strong, however, and soon we found that she had built a nest in a nearby wild raspberry patch and was laying eggs. The discovery was not limited to us; again a predator raided the nest and partook of the eggs. This Mrs. Duck gave up, her broody mood broken by two futile attempts to start a family. There came a day when the second Mrs. Duck couldn't be seen at the pond and didn't appear all day. We made a thorough search of the area hoping that she had started a nest, but there was no trace of her.

Now we feared that our fox friend or some other predator had made a dinner of our duck. Mr. Drake seemed to mope around the pond, lost, one of his mates vanished.

It was a thrilling day when I heard an excited shout from Kay. "Come quick, Jim! Look at what's coming down the driveway!"

There, waddling down the gravel driveway, her head thrust proudly in the air, making soft, soothing sounds was the missing Mrs. Duck. She was followed by a procession of twelve fluffy multicolored ducklings, their little legs and webbed feet churning as they attempted to keep up with their mother. Down the steep slope they paraded, across the yard-lawn, down over the bank to the lower lawn, and down the path to the pond, Mrs. Duck never missing a step, the ducklings tripping and scrambling as they followed her crooning voice.

Mr. Drake didn't seem at all surprised at this turn of events. He didn't hesitate to dunk a couple of his children with his bill until driven away by an irate Mrs. Duck.

We later found out that this Mrs. Duck, frustrated by her companion's attempts to start a family near the pond, had gone further afield to find a more secure location. She found it on the upper side of the highway where there is a piece of marshy ground, a close source of food and water but not a great swimming hole. She made her nest, laid her eggs, then brooded them until the clutch hatched. As soon as the ducklings could make a trip, it was back to the old pond.

That wasn't the end of Mrs. Duck's loyalty to her nesting home. Every so often she would take off up the driveway followed by her ducklings, marching in single file, across the field of hay, her babies lost from sight but following her voice as she gave directions, across the hardtop highway, through brushes and bramble to her old nesting site. They would have a short visit and then reverse the march and return to the pond. These excursions became so frequent that we feared for the safety of our feathered friends as they crossed the highway. Grandson Marshall took matters into his own hands, painted a sign "Ducks Crossing," and erected it at the spot Mrs. Duck and her children always used to cross Route 103.

I was startled one evening when a car dusted down the driveway and stopped by my side. "I think your duck has been struck by a car," John Winslow said. "She's flopping around in the grass just off the shoulder of the road and seems to be hurt."

To this day I'm not sure that I took the time to thank John for coming down to the house to give me the bad news. I was in shock as I ran up the driveway to the side of the highway. Mrs. Duck was hurt, badly hurt, and was doing herself no good as she thrashed around in the grass in obvious pain, afraid of strange people, worried about her babies. John looked on with concern as I went to the side of the crippled bird.

We never did learn the identity of the hit-and-run driver. My anger has not lessened. How could anyone miss seeing a large duck and a string of small ones as they crossed the hardtop. He or she may have been driving too fast to see the "Ducks Crossing" sign, too fast to avoid hitting Mrs. Duck, but they couldn't have hit her and not known it happened.

I picked Mrs. Duck up as gently as I could, holding her wings to prevent any further damage and returned to the house. The duck-lings followed me down the driveway in single file and continued past the house to the pond to join Mr. Drake and the other Mrs. Duck.

They never made the trip back to their birthing home again. Meanwhile, as I examined the injured Mrs. Duck I wished fervently that Kay was home instead of away for a few days.

I am hopeless and helpless when it comes to tending the sick, whether it be humans, animals or birds. I didn't have to be a medical expert to see that Mrs. Duck had received major injuries, probably fatal. I wrapped her in a towel to prevent her from using her wings, one of which was badly damaged, made a bed in a box with soft cloths for a mattress, and tried to make her as comfortable as possible. She looked at me with soulful eyes and made soft sounds, as if thanking me for my tender care. I offered her a drink in a saucer and she sipped it gratefully. I left her to do the chores and when I returned a few hours later she had died.

Mr. Drake didn't know what had happened to his mate, unless the ducklings were able to convey the bad news, but he adapted well to the situation, offering protection and, I suppose, some instruction on how to live and survive at Twin Pines Farm. We kept our water poultry that winter, putting them up in the shed that had once served as a stable. You cannot comprehend the full meaning of messy until you have fed and watered a flock of ducks over winter. They use their large watering container for both drinking and bathing purposes, splashing water all over their living quarters.

That causes some problems in summer but becomes a major one in winter as water freezes and ice builds up. By spring there was a foot of ice in the area of their watering pan, mixed with hay, straw and feed. Those ducks could hear you from the time you shut the door of the house and started crunching through the snow to the barn. The inconsonant quacking was loud enough to be heard in Hartland or Woodstock, the sound reverberating from the sides of the valley as it travelled up and down the St. John River. We had plenty of duck eggs that spring but no brooders, no ducklings.

The ducks were fun and not too difficult to raise in spite of the natural enemies that lived on the farm. They were a delight, often waddling up the hill to the house to serenade the occupants at first break of day, reminding us that it was time to eat.

We found that our next experiment in feather-husbandry was

more difficult and less rewarding in many ways. I became fascinated with ring-necked pheasants, noted for the gorgeous plumage of the cocks, when I did a story on these birds at the farm of Malcolm (Mac) Haynes in Plymouth. These long-tailed, gallinaceous birds are raised in many parts of Canada and the United States. It is not uncommon to see one in the fields and along roads in Carleton County for many have escaped custody, or been allowed freedom. They are not easily domesticated but can be raised successfully by those with the proper knowledge and patience.

Mac supplied me with a number of pheasant eggs and they were placed in my electric incubator with great care. We had a pretty good hatch and the pheasant chicks provided a few surprises that called for immediate action. First, they were so tiny that the standard chicken wire couldn't hold them. They are quick on their feet and we thought we had hatched a brood of the famous cartoon roadrunners, the way they darted around the pen and out through the holes in the wire. A second pen was hastily built, this one with much smaller holes in the wire. The yellow and brown chicks grew quickly and lost none of their speed.

Next we bought a beautiful ring-necked pheasant cock from Mac to ride herd of this flock of chicks, a mixture of hens and cocks. We had to build a special pen for them off the hen house, including a wire roof — both to protect them from hawks and to keep them from flying to freedom.

We also built them their own quarters in the hen house to keep them separated from their feathered friends. A special shelter in their yard gave them shade and a roost for casual snoozing. The next spring came and some of the young cocks were starting to flex their muscles, to preen and show off their magnificent plumage. Still, no eggs were laid. One morning I went over to feed the poultry and our handsome cock was on his side in the pheasant yard, stone dead. We gave up on the experiment and released the remainder of the pheasants to the woods at Twin Pines Farm, back to their natural habitat. We eventually dispersed our hen and duck flocks, neighbor Harry Tibbits becoming the owner of a ragtag variety of poultry of many shapes and colors.

13

Pied Piper of Twin Pines

Animal husbandry is not my forté. It was son Bruce who introduced us to adventures in keeping animals. He was a veritable Pied Piper of Twin Pines Farm. I'm not sure where it all started, with pigs, goats, chickens or cattle. I do recall clearly that they would all follow him anywhere on the farm, a mighty strange procession to see.

Mrs. Pig was probably the first of his domestic menagerie, so called because he was in the habit of letting them run wild. She had a home, of course, a building moved below the slope and in close-proximity to the old apple tree on the lower lawn. This was the building that later became home for the Meat Kings. Mrs. Pig was quite content in her sturdy wooden building, a pole fence giving her a good yard in which to get exercise. Contrary to the belief of many non-country folk, pigs are very clean animals. They make their toilet in a specific place chosen for such chores and do not foul their own homes unless given no other choice. They do like to wallow in mud and choose a spot for that if one can be found or created. They like people if given the opportunity, though they are easily spooked until they become used to their handlers.

Mrs. Pig had her home and her yard but she was allowed the run of the farm when Bruce was working outside. She would follow him wherever he went, snorting and grunting in contentment, pushing her solid snout into the grass or ground, snuffling as she tried to find tidbits for a snack. It was a strange sight. Mrs. Pig had become a pet.

Bruce also brought home the first of our cattle, a young red-brown steer. It was only logical that he be named Mr. Steer. Bruce was challenged to test that old myth that people can build their strength by lifting a heifer or steer clear of the ground daily. The animal gains weight each day and as it grows the lift becomes more difficult. The theory is that the lifter gains strength each day too and can keep up with the growth of the liftee. Not so! Bruce was always strong and pumped iron at one time to further develop his strength. We kept no records on Mr. Steer's weight when it finally became too much for Bruce's lifting power, but that day finally came. The liftee was winner over the lifter.

Mr. Steer was treated much the same as Mrs. Pig, allowed to roam within reason, and invited to accompany Bruce when he went for walks in the woods. Having cattle means the building of fences, unless you're going to keep them in the stable with only an attached corral to allow them to exercise, or chain-tether them to an iron stake, options Bruce would not even consider.

Fence building and fence maintenance are the bane of all farmers and ranchers. We started out with a barbed wire fence of two strands enclosing about four acres of pasture and woods, running from the house east to the river, then south, uphill west and north, an irregular rectangle that offered both grass and the shade of trees. An old bathtub salvaged from the ruins of the former house was buried inside the pasture, near to the house, and was fed water from the old well, or could be filled by a hose.

The next animals to arrive were goats, Trixie and Pixie, the four legged clowns of Twin Pines Farm. They quickly won the hearts of all concerned, being loving, mischievous, feisty, curious and individualistic. They were constantly getting into trouble, worse than any two-year-old child. This was particularly true because Bruce let them have the run of the place most of the time. One day Bruce had to go to Woodstock and left Trixie and Pixie roaming loose. He thought he had closed and locked the door to the house. The two goats didn't waste any time investigating the possibilities. Somehow or other they were able to get the door open, entered the house and browsed around at their leisure. When we did get home the goats had left the house, but not before devouring every house plant they could reach, cropping them right to the earth. The one exception was a Jerusalem

Cherry tree, our pride and joy for many years. We've often wondered how the goats knew that this particular plant is poison.

Bruce now had his followers, in the literal sense, and was ready to act the part of Pied Piper of Twin Pines. Off he would go for a stroll in the woods, to break trails or widen those already there, and Mrs. Pig, Mr. Steer, Trixie and Pixie and two dogs would follow in single file. It was a picture that is difficult to visualize unless seen with your own eyes.

On one occasion Bruce's father-in-law, Walter Gray of Jacksontown, was part of a crew picking fiddleheads at Twin Pines Farm, down along the bank of the St. John River.

"How you doing, Walter?" Bruce asked, scuffing through the spring freshet-tangled long grass of the bank.

"I'd be doing a heck of a lot better if it wasn't for that consarned pig of yours," Walter replied. "It seems that every time I find a good spot to do some fiddleheading that darned pig pushes her snout in and starts eating. I wish you'd leave her home!"

That was too much to ask. Bruce seldom kept the animals restrained when he was working around the farm. He would go and they would follow. There was a price to be paid. When Mrs. Pig finally went to market she was not Grade 1 meat. She was too lean, from all of her running around, and too muscular (tough meat). Mr. Steer didn't go to market that first fall. He wintered over in the barn, getting bigger by the day, and spent the next summer in pasture.

Mr. Steer turned out to be a beautiful animal, big and strong. He was too powerful, too unpredictable to be allowed the freedom of his first summer. He had to be kept in pasture and the day came when even Bruce had difficulty controlling him, if Mr. Steer had ideas of his own. He too went to market but in top condition.

Bruce may have had a good old time "playing" with his domesticated animals — the pig, steer and goats — but he had much less luck with a dog he was keeping for a friend, an Irish Setter. Here was a playful animal that became a killer, despite its intentions. There was a day when we allowed our hens and roosters to range over the farm, pecking and scratching as they hunted for bugs and insects. The Irish Setter put an end to that practice. He wanted to play war games with all of those noisy, feathered creatures, strongly believing that his role in life was the chasing of all birds, large or small, even unto death. He was good at his job! Hen after hen fell before his attacks. A good many solutions were tried but none of them worked. These included tying a dead hen around his neck where it flopped as he ran, and kept him a constant companion until it dropped off. The killing continued and finally the Irish Setter had to be moved to a different location where he wouldn't be tantalized and teased by the sight of running hens. Peace was restored at Twin Pines Farm. Our own dog, Mollie, did not chase hens. She was their pal.

Bruce's empathy with animals may or may not have been a good omen for a would-be farmer. As most farmers will aver, cows, pigs, horses and goats are not pets. They are kept for a purpose and, eventually, all but the horses will be sent to market to provide meat for the home or for sale. Even horses meet that fate in some countries though horse steaks and roasts have never achieved wide popularity in New Brunswick. Whether he was too soft with animals or not, Bruce was at one time determined to become a farmer. This was back in those "silly season" days when federal and provincial agriculture departments struggled to get rid of as much taxpayers money as possible, a policy that led to hundreds of farm bankruptcies in the years to follow. Bruce almost became one of those tragic statistics.

When he talked to Kay and me about farming as a career, Bruce was dreaming, as we all do, but was it an impossible dream? Not really, even if it proved so for Bruce. Our 45-acre farm was too small for full-time traditional farming if you wanted to make a living; not enough acres for potatoes or grain, not sufficient pasture for raising beef or dairy cattle, no large barns and machine sheds, no potato house, no horses, tractors or machinery. This was a major stumbling block. However, it was large enough to consider several options, including strawberries, raspberries, tree farming and commercial greenhouses. Bruce made a study of these long before they reached the level of popularity they have achieved today.

The problem was money. We were in no position to raise cash for Bruce's projects, having quite enough of a financial load ourselves.

He was living at home and that took care of room and board. He had become involved in husbandry in a small way. There was land that could be used. What was needed was "seed" money, sufficient to purchase supplies to build one or two greenhouses, for starters, and to buy the necessary equipment, such as furnaces, pipes and pumps for feeding and watering plants in the greenhouses, and to purchase plants from nurseries. Bruce worked a pencil to the wood as he estimated the cost of his project, the minimum he would need to get launched.

My self-inflicted role was to obtain as much technical and financial information as possible, since as a journalist I had many good contacts in numerous fields of endeavor. I also knew many provincial MLAs and federal MPs and was certain they could help me get the information we needed, including financial programs for farmers at both levels of government. When I put the matter to Robert (Bob) Howie, then MP for York-Sunbury, he suggested that Bruce have a talk with one of the staff of the federal department responsible for aid to farmers. He arranged such a meeting in Fredericton. Bruce and I went to Elm City confident that the goal was within reach. Bob not only arranged the meeting but he was there to add at least spiritual support, a subtle reminder to the federal bureaucrat that the MP had our interests at heart. We had done our homework, eliminating such clearly impractical alternatives as dairy or beef herds, large-scale potato growing, those elements of farming that called for huge capital outlays for machinery, buildings and stock. Bruce had obtained numerous government publications on establishing commercial greenhouses, studied market possibilities, figured out costs and needs. His target was a farm loan of $10,000 to $15,000, enough to get started. This would be sufficient, we thought, as he already had a home, some outbuildings, and could work in the woods in the off season to make a few bucks until his greenhouses provided an income.

After the four of us enjoyed a pleasant lunch, Bob and I carried on a conversation of times past and what was going on in the world while Bruce and the bureaucrat got into the nitty gritty of the purpose of the meeting. I could not help but overhear some of the conversation and was amazed at the trend it was taking. Bruce's modest proposal was greeted with disdain. It was suggested that he should ask for $200,000 or even $250,000 and tackle a major farm operation. The government was not interested in marginal operations, in supporting subsistence farmers. Big is beautiful, Bruce was told. Buy more land, get heavily into growing potatoes, or start a dairy or beef herd, erect buildings, buy heavy tractors and equipment. That's the type of operation the government would support.

He almost sold Bruce on the idea, too. On the return drive to Wakefield I posed some questions that Bruce would have to answer himself. If, for example, he did receive a $200,000 loan from the government, how would he make the interest payments of at least $20,000 a year, possibly $2,000 a month? It would take time, years probably, before he could see any income from his big farming operation. How could he make any payments? He was talking full-time farming that would leave no possibility of earning money by working in the woods during the winter. Was there any chance his request for $10,000 or $15,000 would be accepted? The answer was "no." Forget it, I advised, you'd be biting off more than you can chew and bankruptcy would surely be the ultimate result.

The project was abandoned and I'm still not certain I gave the right advice for the times. However, years later interest rates soared above twenty per cent and wiped out many farmers across Canada, particularly those who had been prodded by bureaucrats into taking huge government loans that imposed a financial burden the farmers couldn't carry even in good times. Ironically, Bruce has an uncle, Ben Baldwin of Douglasfield, who has carried on Bruce's dream in recent years. Ben, who has his doctorate in geology, returned to his old homestead after the death of his father, Harold, a few years ago. He had not farmed since university days three decades earlier.

The Baldwin spread at Douglasfield, a few miles from Chatham, was declared a Pioneer Farm in 1967, meaning it had been in the same family for at least 100 years. When Ben returned there to live he found an antique tractor that still worked, machinery still capable of doing a job, a well-maintained big barn and machine buildings, and a lot of acres of good, flat land. He too studied the alternatives and opted for market gardening rather than cattle or one large crop such as potatoes. He decided to build a greenhouse and raise tomatoes, cucumbers and lettuce. The first was a success and he built a second. In addition, he now plants many acres of corn and potatoes, sufficient to provide produce for his stand at the farmers' market in Newcastle each week, as well as a brisk "farm gate" sale during the summer months. He's making it work, but Ben is no Pied Piper, he's a realist.

Twin Pines Farm lost its Pied Piper when Bruce abandoned his dream of a career of farming. No more will we see a man taking a stroll in the woods, followed by a pig, steer, goats and two dogs. It was great fun while it lasted.

14

Goats Are Great Kidders

"What's that on the hood of my car?" Harold Baldwin roared as he looked out the kitchen window. Kay's parents had come to Twin Pines Farm for a visit and hadn't been in the house for more than two minutes when I heard his indignant roar.

I didn't have to look out the window to know the cause of his anger. It was just a matter of which goat it was: Trixie or Pixie — the brown and white Toggenburg or the white Saanen. It was Trixie the Togg.

Our adventures with goats began when Bruce brought the two pranksters to the farm. By now Kay and I were convinced that goats are the most lovable creatures that can be found on a farm, though there are all too few goat farmers in New Brunswick.

I hurried out the door and shooed Trixie off the hood of Dad's car, thus restoring harmony to the visit, for a time at least. It wouldn't be long before either Trixie or Pixie returned to the hood of Harold's car, or perhaps ours. Goats love to climb on top of anything that is above ground. They are great kidders, in more ways than one, quick to see an opportunity to get into mischief of some kind.

This predilection for mischief is in their genes, a hereditary trait from the time when their ancestors scampered sure footed on mountain crags and peaks. That is just one of their endearing qualities. They also love people, get along with other animals (including pets) and are practical providers. Goats supply milk that is in some ways superior to that from cows; they supply meat, known as chevon, for those who enjoy it; their hides are made into fantastic leather.

I tried to explain this to Harold as we stood in the yard and watched Trixie and Pixie frolic around the yard looking for some other mischief that might appeal to them, casting an occasional glance at the two cars. They knew there was fun to be had climbing on cars. Pixie had destroyed the plastic grill on the front of our new car just days after I took delivery because the rungs would not support her weight as she scaled her mountain to stand on top of the vehicle's roof.

Harold was not convinced of the sterling character of our goats. He had lived and worked on a farm all of his life and knew more about horses, cattle and hogs than I ever will. He was convinced that goats had no claim to fame as legitimate livestock, that they had no rightful place on a "real" farm, a prejudice shared by many of his peers to this day. Most farmers will not consider raising goats; they won't even consider them as a possible family pet.

Kay and I were just as convinced that goats are the darlings of any farm on which they do live. Toggs and Saanens are just two of the five most popular breeds raised in Canada and the United States, though all of them originated in other countries.

We learned that Nubians, easily identified by their pendulous ears, are the most numerous in North America, though they give less milk than other breeds. Their ancestry is traced to India and Egypt. The French Alpine, usually white and black, originated in the Alps. Toggenburgs, the oldest registered breed in the world, came from Switzerland where herd records date back to the 1600s. The Saanen is also Swiss in origin, named for the Saanen Valley. They are always white and are renowned as the "Holstein" of the goat world, being the heaviest milkers. The fifth breed, LaMancha, is an almost earless animal, a fairly "new" addition to the goat world. Two other breeds deserve mention because of their rapid rise in popularity, the Angora (raised for mohair and meat) and the African Pygmy (21 inches tall, or less, at the withers), an excellent milker.

When Bruce abandoned his plans to become a full-time farmer and started his search for another career, Kay and I became the apprehensive owners of Trixie and Pixie. That meant watering and feeding, trying to fence them in, milking, getting them bred each year, and reducing their shenanigans to an acceptable level, a challenge willing accepted as we adopted these rapscallions.

Goats Are Great Kidders

The fencing-in was an almost impossible job. The fenced cattle pasture wouldn't even start to hold them; they easily jumped over the top wire, disregarding the possible danger of the strand of barbed wire to their huge, low-slung udders.

We electrified the pasture fence, strung a long connecting wire across to a newly erected goat pasture behind the barn, and were convinced we now had a way to keep Trixie and Pixie in their field. We even erected a shelter in the middle of their pasture, a refuge from hot sun, rain and wind. We badly underestimated the cunning and agility of our goats. They escaped from the electrified enclosure whenever they wanted to do so. They didn't go far, just roamed around the nearby field, visited the garden to taste the offerings, and usually ended up around the house, waiting for either Kay or me to come out and play. Goats love to play!

We soon learned that the old stories about goats eating tin cans, or anything else they encounter, were nothing but malicious myths. Goats are browsers, like deer, and love to nibble at the green leaves of trees. They can reach at least six feet when standing on their hind legs and will prune the greenery from a tree in a perfect circle. Trixie and Pixie lost no time in doing so in their new pasture where alders were found in profusion.

Goats are fastidious eaters; we discovered just how fastidious they are in their eating habits when we assumed the responsibility of putting them in the barn each night, to be fed, milked, and bedded down. Each goat had her own stall, with a large teardrop hole in the door so they could reach out to get their hay and grain. When they dropped hay on the floor, they wouldn't touch it again.

Milking was done by hand at Twin Pines Farm, as it is at most goat farms in the province. We have a raised milking stand for the animal which makes it easier to get at the job and allows the goat to munch on grain while being milked. The Toggs have large teats, the Saanens much smaller ones. Since Kay and I had both spent years on farms we were not intimidated at the prospect of milking goats but we did discover we used different techniques. Kay is a squeezer; I'm a stripper. If using the former style, you wrap your fingers around the two teats (goats have only two) and squeeze, and if you do it properly and the goat is amenable, a stream of rich white milk foams into the pail. In the stripping technique, thumb and forefinger are curled around the teat near the udder and then pressure applied by the other fingers, one at a time in sequence, and this stripping action again produces a stream of milk — if the goat wants to let it down. We never have figured out which technique is the best though Kay could get more from Trixie and Pixie than I could.

We were not in the goat business too long before we were faced with the responsibility of having our two nannies bred. Goats, like cows, will give milk only so long after they have given birth. Cows produce calves; goats produce kids. A breeding program is a must on any farm where animals and poultry are raised. There's no problem with hens. Put a rooster or two in the yard and duty will be done. Fertile eggs will be laid and if you don't have a fancy incubator, the hens will set on the nest and chickens will eventually break out of the eggs. In fact, broody hens will gather a clutch of eggs and set even if you do have an incubator. It's not that easy with goats, or other animals. You have to be able to detect when the nannies are ready for breeding, when they are in heat. That's because goats owners do not as a rule allow a billy (male) to run with the nannies.

We discovered why when we took Trixie and Pixie to be serviced, at the same time learning why many uninformed people keep repeating the myth that goats give off an odor that is unpleasant, to say the least. We had wondered about this because Trixie and Pixie, though not smelling of roses, did not give off an obnoxious odor. They were clean animals. Billy goats are something else again, particularly during the mating season. They do give off an offensive odor. They stink! Small wonder they are kept to themselves.

Our first breeding session with a billy not only informed us about the origin of the myth about smelly goats, it also introduced us to what must be one of the briefest courtships in the animal kingdom. A billy doesn't waste any time in foreplay. We always thought that roosters were quick to get the job done; I believe billies are just as fast, perhaps faster. If the nanny is biologically ready for pregnancy the billy acts immediately he is in the presence of his short-term bride. If you've misjudged the situation it is back to the farm and try again another day. The same is true if the first mating doesn't take; try, try again. For a short time after a breeding session the nanny will probably have a repulsive odor emanating from her coat, the result of close contact with the billy, but this will soon disappear after exposure to fresh air in the pasture.

Kay and I were becoming more interested in goats as each day passed and we became familiar with their lovable traits, and those not so lovable. The worst that could be said of Trixie and Pixie was that they were too full of life, too mischievous at times. They were wonderful milk producers, milk that could be used to make a remarkable cheese. We wondered if they would be good mothers. Goats don't always produce just one kid. Often they have twins or triplets, even quadruplets. We learned more about the animals, their good points and bad, as we talked with other owners, joined organizations and obtained literature and books.

This keen interest in goats led us to the Westmorland County Fair in Petitcodiac one year, an annual event that draws goat owners from all parts of the province, as well as from Nova Scotia and Prince Edward Island. It is a show and sale, promising that you can see the best of the goat breeds in the Maritimes and take the opportunity to upgrade your own stock.

"There's no way I'm going to be suckered into buying any more goats," I cautioned Kay as we prepared to make the trip to Petitcodiac. Grandson Doug was to accompany us because he loved Trixie and Pixie and wanted to see what other breeds of goats would be at the show. "I'm going to take just enough money for gasoline and for lunch for the three of us, then I won't be tempted to buy anything."

Kay agreed that his would be a wise policy, knowing all too well that her husband is an impulse buyer, quick to reach for the pocketbook if he sees something he wants.

The Westmorland show proved to be an even more exciting adventure than we had hoped for. The best of goats from many parts of the Maritimes were on display, with P.E.I. owners taking many of the ribbons for their entries. We saw Nubians and French Alpines for the first time, and a few LaManchas. The Toggs and Saanens were spectacular, though we thought Trixie and Pixie would have done well in competition against them if our terrible two were groomed to show standards.

When we first entered the arena at Petitcodiac my eyes had been attracted to a pair of white and black French Alpine kids tethered at one exhibitor's space. "It's a good thing we didn't bring our money, Kay," I said, pointing to the Alpine twins, "I'd probably buy them if I had."

"Yield not to temptation," Kay replied, quickly leading Doug and me away to look at other sights and spectacles. We were all impressed with the quality of the livestock and with the judging of the animals, learning at first hand what the judges were looking for in the different breeds. My attention, however, kept straying; I couldn't get the Alpine twins off my mind and returned to see them, talk to them and pet them, again and again. The owner was not in the least reluctant to quote a price for the two female kids, extolling their virtues and bragging of the lineage of their parents.

After we had lunched on hot dogs and hamburgers and had our coffee and cold drinks, I suggested to Kay that the two Alpine kids would be a valuable addition to our herd, expanding it by one hundred per cent at one stroke. I could see that she liked them too and Doug was wildly enthusiastic about the prospect of buying them.

"Perhaps we could go down town to the bank and draw out the money," I suggested.

"They don't know you here. I doubt very much if they would do it," Kay said, but agreed that it was worth a try.

At first the bank refused to advance us the money. They didn't know us, we hadn't brought passbook or cheque book with us, and the identification cards we did carry would not move them from their position. "How about using our credit card?" I asked in desperation. That did it. Plastic magic had worked again. In no time at all the cash was in my hands and we were headed back to the arena. Not too long after that we were headed back for Wakefield, our goat herd now twice as large as when we left home.

Goats Are Great Kidders

We had not taken our pickup with us, another ploy to keep me from going wild and purchasing more goats. We figured it would be almost impossible to return with any animals as there would be insufficient room in the car. Never allow reality to interfere with a dream.

I was puzzled at first when cars would pass us, their occupants craning their necks to get a peek inside our vehicle, then faces breaking out in wide grins. When I looked in the rear view mirror I could see what they were smiling about. We had managed to pilfer a piece of plastic to put over the back seat and the floor of the car, just in case the kids had an "accident" on the way home. As I looked in the mirror I could see Doug sitting in the middle of the back seat. On each side, sitting proudly, with heads high, were the two beautiful kids, taking a great interest in the passing scenery and quite at home in their new surroundings.

The trip home was uneventful except for the attention paid to our passengers by people in passing cars. It was probably the topic of conversation at many dinner tables that night, a story likely met with hoots of disbelief. Goats do not sit up in seats — and who would think of taking such "smelly" animals into a car in the first place.

Our herd continued to grow over the next few years, with Trixie and Pixie as the seniors, each producing one or two kids every spring. This brought a new chore to the farm, that of bottle-feeding the kids. The baby goats are usually taken from their mothers as soon as they are born and bottle fed. That's hand labor for the person chosen for the task. It means holding one, two or more kids and allowing them to suck at the special nipples on bottles of warm goat milk. It is not an unpleasant chore. Indeed, it is a very rewarding one because kids bring out the best in a person, the warmth and tenderness usually reserved for human babies. One spring we were bottle-feeding seven kids. Our herd had grown to eleven.

The part about building a herd that did concern us was the fact that, like humans, goats are unpredictable when it comes to the gender of their offspring. Some years there would be more male kids than female, other years it would be the opposite. The male kids were a big problem. They are of no value to a herd as most owners try to avoid inbreeding and do not want a breeding billy from their own stock.

Certainly, herds of our size or smaller need only one billy and it is usually preferable to take your nanny to another goat owner to upgrade the quality of your herd. Some like to experiment, to cross Toggs with Saanens or Alpines, or some other mix, but most prefer to achieve as pure a specific strain as possible, particularly if they plan to show their animals. For example, one of our young goats — Dixie — was the offspring of Pixie and a pure Saanen billy. Dixie went on to win ribbons at shows in future years, after we had dispersed our herd.

Since Kay and I did not plan to raise any billy goats the problem became similar to that of people whose cat has produced a litter of unwanted kittens. What to do with them? We are not great lovers of chevon (goat meat), nor did we plan to raise our young male goats, butcher them and sell the meat. The answer was to sell them to somebody who did want male kids.

We did what other goat owners in the Maritimes do in such a case: we sold them to a dealer from Quebec who makes a regular circuit through the Maritimes to purchase goats and other livestock. Though chevon is not in great demand in New Brunswick as a meat, it is popular in ethnic communities in Quebec and Ontario. This is particularly true in the spring of the year, the time when the majority of kids are born. You don't make a great deal of money by selling male kids or other goats for meat but it is sufficient to help meet the feed bill.

Actually, there's no real money for the average owner in raising goats. The successful breeder can build a herd to the size that it will at least break even financially by continually upgrading stock, improving milk production, winning honors at goat shows around the Maritimes, and earning the reputation of having superior stock in specific breeds, such as Toggenburg and Saanen, or French Alpine. The situation changed in 1988 with a goat dairy becoming a reality in the Maritimes. Goat farmers now had a place where they could legitimately sell their milk and be assured of an income from this product. There is a demand for goat milk. It can often be used by people allergic to cow's milk. The trouble had been that it could be sold only at the farm gate because it was not pasteurized and thus did not meet health regulations. The advent of a dairy to process goat milk gave assurance that health regulations would be met. The result may be larger goat herds in the Maritimes and more farm owners getting into this growing industry.

The truth is that most goat owners in the Maritimes have raised these unpredictable animals more for the love of having them around than for commercial gain. That's the way it was at Twin Pines Farm. We did build the herd up to eleven and did upgrade our stock considerably, but not to make money. We enjoyed having them around, utterly fascinated with their antics, their mischief making.

The goat (*capra hircus*) has been called "the poor man's cow" with good reason. A dairy goat, not much bigger than a large dog, can produce up to 4,000 pounds of milk during a year (depending on the breed), does not require large living quarters, is less costly to feed than a cow, gets along well with people and other animals, and quickly becomes part of the family. They enjoy company so many owners insist on having at least two goats.

We started out with two but then our affection for this animal overcame our common sense and we ended up with eleven, Trixie and Pixie remaining our favorites. It was a sad day when we dispersed the herd as we prepared to leave the farm and move West. We came back to Twin Pines, of course, but we have never returned to raising goats. Other dreams took priority.

15
The Last Roundup

Attention was on the dais at the front of the ring as auctioneer Dow Foster called for the next animal at the weekly sale of livestock at the Carleton Co-Operatives Ltd. barn at Florenceville. As usual the steep-tiered grandstand seats were filled to capacity with area farmers, representatives of abattoirs from New Brunswick and Quebec, and interested onlookers. Cattle are the mainstay of the auction but Dow Foster's familiar "cry" also disposes of horses, hogs, goats and ponies. The auction is a weekly tradition for many who come to buy, sell or observe.

Robert and I were there to buy. With Bruce and Mr. Steer both gone from Twin Pines Farm, we decided we would get into cattle raising in a small way. At first we purchased from a local farmer. The next year we decided to go the auction route, perhaps four animals. We would each have one for our freezers; the other two would be sold as meat, hopefully for a price that would help pay the cost of our steers, including the purchase of grain, salt licks for the pasture and continued maintenance of electric fencing.

We can blame Bruce for this mad experiment. If he hadn't bought Mr. Steer and kept him at the farm through two summers, we probably wouldn't have ever tried to get into the cattle business. Mr. Steer had produced more than good meat; he had an entertainment value that cannot be dismissed, as well as a hint of danger. In my opinion, cattle are about the dumbest of all domesticated creatures, not easy to train and balky at the best of times. Mr. Steer was different, almost a pet. He would follow Bruce on his walks through the woods and around the farm, loved to be petted and talked to, and added visual cosmetics to the pastoral scene — a reddish brown hulking beauty in a sea of green grass, the blue of the St. John River in the background.

The Last Roundup

He was friendly, too friendly, as he grew and grew. When anyone entered his pasture Mr. Steer would arrive immediately, pushing not too gently with his head. It was difficult for Mr. Steer to be gentle because of his size and weight. A nudge could send you sprawling.

I can still hear Kay's plaintive call for help as she went into the pasture to gather apples from a huge old tree, with Mr. Steer giving her playful pushes with his powerful head all the way. I interceded on her behalf, getting his attention and calling him away. It was also Mr. Steer who taught Kay the right and wrong way to get through an electric fence, a skill all must learn on the farm.

The day of Kay's shocking experience she had gone to the barn and returned with a bucket of grain to feed the steer. She approached the fence with some trepidation, knowing full well the jolt that can be expected if you're not careful. Kay carefully pushed the bucket through the top and bottom strands of electric wire and set it on the ground in the pasture. Then she warily reached one leg and foot through the two strands, holding onto the top of the bucket with both hands to maintain her balance as she started to draw her other leg through the opening. Unfortunately, she raised her butt at the same time and it came in contact with the top strand of electrified fence. The resulting jolt, well grounded through her body and the pail, sent the container of grain hurtling in one direction and Kay in another. She sustained no major injuries but the adventure did bruise her feelings for awhile and Mr. Steer, being the handiest, took most of the blame.

Our experience with Mr. Steer and subsequent animals had also taught us that we should have a corral to temporarily hold cattle when bringing them home or loading them for departure. It gives them a chance to calm down and makes the job much easier. Cattle are easily spooked, as we were to learn the hard way. That's why we had constructed a corral at the pasture's gate entrance before going to the auction at Florenceville. We wanted to be prepared.

To give the devil his due, the corral had been built by Robert and Ben Baldwin. The idea was to have a holding pen we could unload the cattle into; they would remain there for awhile to get over the trauma of an open ride in the back of a pickup, have a chance to eat some hay and grain and look over their new pasture, and get acclimatized.

It was a wonderful theory, one that should prevent the cattle from getting spooked when they were unloaded from the half-ton. That's what we thought as we sat in the grandstand at the Co-Op auction barn in Florenceville and watched and listened to Dow Foster's hypnotic chant as he extolled the virtues of bob calves, milch cows, feeder calves, steers and bulls, heifers, horses, ponies and an evil looking white billy goat. Robert and I are not cattle people. We both know a Holstein from a Jersey, a Hereford from a Black Angus, and we had been told that many of the dairy-beef crosses are a good buy. We ended up with four animals that probably no one else wanted, a motley looking herd that, we hoped, would turn out to be exceedingly healthy and fit after a summer in pasture, topped off with a month of grain feeding. They were of various sizes, colors and crossbreeding, one being a fairly large heifer with a lot of Holstein in her blood.

We drew a collective sigh of relief as I backed the pickup to the corral gate, three poles that could be slipped aside to allow the cattle through. What I didn't know is that a similar gate at the other end of the corral hadn't been set properly. The frightened cattle had to be pushed off the tailgate of the pickup into the enclosure, a procedure that did nothing to settle their nerves. Bellowing over the indignities imposed on them they milled about seeking some means of escape from the pen. We stood and watched the melee with smug satisfaction, looking like the cowboys we were not as we leaned on the top rail of the corral, me lighting a cigarette and Robert puffing on one of his favorite cigars. I'd even worn my stetson for the occasion. The smug look didn't last long.

The largest of the animals took only a few minutes to discover the weakness of the corral and used her head to push aside two of the bars at the pasture-end of the enclosure. The spooked animals took off like a runaway train, following the largest of the herd who had assumed the role of leader. Off across the pasture they stampeded, towards the fence on the other side. They didn't stop. Neither barbed wire nor electric fence would halt their mad charge. They escaped and a hectic roundup followed. We were finally successful in getting the four back into the pasture and the fence repaired.

They stayed in the pasture for several days, seemingly content, calming down and getting used to their new surroundings at Wakefield. Certainly the grazing was excellent, the pond offered easy access to water, and they kept a discreet distance from the fence as if they remembered both the barbs and the electric jolts. We were standing on the deck of the house one morning admiring the cattle in the pasture when something spooked them. Led by the largest of the four, they started to race around the pasture in obvious fear.

We ran into the pasture and tried to calm them down, talking to them soothingly, imploring them to take it easy. It was not to be. The leader made an end run around us, raced to the lower side of the pasture and, subduing any painful memories of barbs and electric shock, crashed through the south fence and made her escape. She was followed by her three companions despite our efforts to keep them from getting to the breached fence. This time, being at the bottom of the hill, they took to the cover of the nearby woods — and disappeared. We spent hours in a fruitless search, six or more people trying to find the missing cattle. We hadn't located them by nightfall, nor were we any more successful the following morning.

The mystery of the missing cattle was not solved for several days. Had they turned and gone upriver through the woods? Had they gone downriver? Did they swim the St. John River and gain sanctuary on the other side? We thought we had looked in every possible direction.

One day we received a phone call saying that our AWOL cattle were believed to be mixed in with Harry Tibbits' herd, several fields south of Twin Pines Farm. We checked and sure enough, there they were, grazing contentedly with Harry's herd, though all together as if maintaining their own unit within a larger one. We made a half-hearted effort to separate them and start a cattle drive back to our place but they were too spooky. We decided we needed more cowboys and cowgirls for a successful roundup to get the four deserters and called upon some of Robert's friends to come out and earn their spurs, *sans* horses. The roundup was set for a Saturday and was to be a real country frolic, the hard work to be followed by a cold drink and a feast. Someone forgot to send the missing cattle an invitation. They wouldn't cooperate. We took it easy, trying to herd them gently in the direction we wanted them to go. Harry had a corral in his pasture for just that purpose, to hold the animals until they could be loaded for transportation, or for a cattle drive up the road. Every time we thought we had them separated from the resident herd and started in the right direction, they'd make an end run around us and escape again. We were physically exhausted after hours of trying to capture the lost herd. Finally, we gave up! At least we knew where the critters were. Harry was kind enough to say that they could run with his herd until the fall roundup — and they did.

Meanwhile, we had also broken into the hog business, purchasing two of the little rascals at the Co-Op auction in Florenceville. Farmers usually arrive with a batch of squealing young pigs in the backs of their pickups, one or two tons, and sell them from the tailgates.

We decided to range our pigs, to allow them to run comparatively free, thus avoiding the work required when you keep them in pens, including disposal of manure. We built a shelter in a small pasture we developed just east of the garden. The only measure taken to keep the pair of porkers from running away was a single strand of electrified fence about six inches above the ground. They were happy in their new home, squealing with delight when we brought them food or came for a visit. They were very clean animals, deciding on one specific spot for their toilet and using it all the time they were with us. They were smart, too. The first time they tried to push their snouts under the electric wire and got a shock was also the last time they tried to escape.

We had never seen hogs range before in this part of the country and didn't quite know what to expect. We thought they would make many attempts to escape, but they were too smart. We didn't know if they would use their roofed shelter when it rained, or as a place to sleep. They were impervious to rain but they did use the shelter for sleeping quarters, both day and night, and to escape the hot sun.

The Last Roundup

What we didn't know was that pigs are as good as a high-priced tiller for turning the soil. They rooted up that pasture from one end to the other, from side to side, during the summer they called it home. The only exception was a narrow band of grass a half-foot from the strand of electric wire. A touch with the harrow and you could have planted that pasture by fall.

Visitors to Twin Pines Farm received more pleasure from watching the pigs plough the pasture with their snouts than they did watching our exotic poultry, or feeding the trout. The two porkers became very much part of the family and we almost dreaded the day they were to be taken to the slaughterhouse. I wasn't at home when the time came, coward that I am, but I'm told it was an hilarious scene as Kay, Beth, Robert and the boys tried to get the now well-developed pigs out of their pasture, up over a steep slope and into the truck. Perhaps they had intuition as to their fate. Whatever it was, they squealed with rage when the crew tackled the job of getting them to the truck. They wouldn't leave the shelter. Then they wouldn't leave their pasture and had to be chased. Carried to the steep slope, they wouldn't climb the hill and had to be forcefully pushed from behind, voicing vehement protest by shrill squealing and harsh grunting as hands prodded their plump hams. The job was finally completed and delivery was made to the slaughterhouse in Jacksonville.

For those who haven't taken animals to a slaughterhouse to have them converted into neat packages of meat, there are some unexpected surprises. When I was a lad on a farm in Avondale, butchering was done at home, whether it involved fowl, cattle or hogs. We decided we would do it the easy way.

The porkers were delivered to the abattoir, as the cattle had been in previous years. Thus we avoided all of the dirty work, the slaughtering, the disposal of unwanted parts, the cutting of carcass into specific roasts and steaks, the grinding of meat, and the wrapping. Theoretically, when you deliver an animal to one of these places you avoid all the nasty hassles involved in butchering. When you get a telephone call saying your meat is ready you arrive to find it all neatly wrapped in butcher's paper, each package clearly marked as to what it contains: roast, chops, steaks, ground meat, etc. — and a bill. The entire operation makes it all seem impersonal, alleviating some of the guilt of having sent a faithful friend and companion to be killed.

You take delivery of the brown paper packages and store them in the freezer, confident that you have at least part of the winter's food at hand. Problems can arise when you start looking for a specific cut of meat and find that the packager has failed to identify what is inside, and it's impossible to ascertain by visual inspection of size and shape.

This resulted in a comic scene one day when Kay went to the freezer to get a fresh (not smoked or cured) ham. Company was expected and we thought it would make an excellent dinner. There is no mistaking the shape of a ham, even if the package isn't marked. Right? Wrong! When the package was brought to the kitchen and unwrapped Kay was looking at a pig's head, not a ham.

When the shock wore off we decided we would try to make a batch of pressed head cheese of which we are fond. We found an excellent recipe in Mildred Trueman's popular collection, *Favourite Recipes from Old New Brunswick Kitchens*, requiring only a pig's head, an onion, a teaspoon of summer savory and salt and pepper to taste. How could anyone go wrong with such a simple recipe? I don't know, but we managed it. The truth is that we never did get a batch of head cheese out of the mess. We don't blame the recipe but we made a mistake somewhere along the line. Nor did we ever find the ham we thought was in the freezer.

We had the same problem with packages of pork and beef from time to time when we would come across a package and try to guess what was inside, and no marking to give us a clue.

Our last roundup at Twin Pines Farm was one I missed. Good neighbor Harry Tibbits, who had kept an eye on our four cattle during the summer, had no trouble at all in rounding them up with his own herd in the fall. Not only that, he trucked them to the abattoir for processing. All we had to do was pick up the boxes of packaged meat. That year was our last attempt at raising hogs and cattle.

16
Cruising Up & Down the River

I had one stipulation when Kay and I first started looking for a site for a permanent home, one we could continue living in after retirement: it must adjoin a body of water — river, lake or ocean. The logical areas to start looking were Carleton County and the Saint John area, since we had roots in both. It was no coincidence that the mighty St. John River is part of the grand history of these two diverse parts of New Brunswick.

This 450-mile river has often been called the "Rhine of America" and was identified as such in advertisements for river boats in the 1800s. It is impossible for the young generation today to realize the important role of the St. John River in New Brunswick's history, providing river transportation from Saint John to Grand Falls before the day of trains and automobiles. This rich history is well recorded in *Steamboat Days On The St. John 1816-1946* by Dr. George MacBeath and Captain Donald F. Taylor. There have been many changes since towboats made regular trips from Fredericton to Woodstock, and from Hartland to the Tobique and up to Grand Falls.

It used to take 3½ to 4½ days for towboats to travel from Fredericton to Woodstock, teams of horses being used to pull the boats through the more difficult stretches of water. The trip down took only 1½ to 2½ days. The introduction of railways sounded the death knell for boat traffic on the St. John, just as steamboats had replaced towboats on the river. Still, it was not until 1948 that the M.S. *D.J. Purdy* made her final voyage downriver from Fredericton to Saint John. I still remember the excitement and spirit of adventure I experienced during trips on both the *Majestic* and the *D.J. Purdy*.

When Kay and I found Twin Pines Farm and discovered that the property included a quarter of a mile frontage on the St. John River, it seemed that the location was an answer to our dreams, particularly mine because of my "need" to be near water, perhaps a result of having served in the Royal Canadian Navy for five years. What we didn't realize at the time was the close historical association between river transportation and the town of Woodstock.

Dr. MacBeath and Capt. Taylor list in their book the names of steamers that plied the St. John River, plus a great deal of other relative information. It is interesting that two of the steamers, *Ben Beveridge* (1853) and the *John Waring* (1852), were built in Woodstock, a town not remembered today as being famed for its shipbuilding. Paradoxically, two of the steamers that were named *Woodstock* were built at shipyards in other centers, one at Portland (Saint John) in 1832, the second at Bath, Maine, in 1852.

There were no steamers running the river when we finally settled in at Twin Pines Farm. The St. John had become a lake from Mactaquac to just above our farm. This NB Power creation has now extended to Hartland, about four miles above Twin Pines, after the head pond was raised again to provide even more low cost electric power for New Brunswickers. The Mactaquac Dam is responsible for wiping out many islands, including the famous Island Park at Woodstock, and even more popular salmon pools, such as the Patterson at Woodstock, the Covered Bridge pool at Hartland, and one just south of Twin Pines Farm.

When we took possession of the farm I already knew there would be no Atlantic salmon fishing just offshore, though previous owners of the property had enjoyed that experience. Now there was a lake with no salmon pool nearby. However, right from the start I had plans for a boat and for fishing. I thought the river could yield a trout at times, as well as bass, pickerel, sun fish, perch and, of course, eels. Twin Pines Farm had several possibilities for water craft, two gullies that could be developed as sheltered landings, and a riverside clearing that would lend itself to establishment of a dock. Such facilities were not part of my dream.

My fleet was started with a Chestnut canoe, a fine craft for a lake, I thought, and adequate for the odd fishing trip on the river. One of my first excursions was a paddle upriver to Hartland and under the celebrated "longest covered bridge in the world." This is a trip of about four miles each way and provides good exercise. It also gives a spectacular view of the St. John River Valley from midstream, thickly wooded shores rising to high hills, scattered homes, barns and outbuildings and cultivated fields. I never fully realized the beauty of Twin Pines Farm until I saw it from the vantage point in my canoe as I paddled the St. John.

It didn't take long to discover that Mactaquac Lake, as many now call it, may look calm at times, but looks can be deceptive. Paddling upriver is an easy run on a tranquil day until you get out of the head pond and into fast water. You get a boost from the fast water on the down river trip until you hit the smooth water of the head pond. What the paddler must never forget is that the St. John River Valley is famous for its winds and they can reach a tremendous force very quickly. When that happens Mactaquac Lake can become a treacherous piece of water for anyone out in a canoe. I've been caught in such conditions while taking a trip from Twin Pines Farm and had to get to shore to avoid disaster. If the wind is from the South, blowing directly upriver, it is almost impossible to paddle the canoe down river against the wind.

The dangers posed by winds to canoeists on Mactaquac Lake were soon learned and guests were always warned of the possibilities, and cautioned to get close to the shore at the first sign of a freshening breeze. We must have done something right because we've had no serious problems with canoeing on the river, nor have our guests.

The nearest we have had to a calamity involved a guest who loves swimming, seizing every opportunity to get into the water. I wasn't at home when she arrived and it being a hot day she and Kay decided to stroll down to the river, our friend expressing a desire for a good swim. Evidently she didn't realize that the part of Mactaquac Lake at our farm was polluted, a stinking mess, the result of sewage and other waste products emptied into the river farther upstream. I had decided after one canoe trip that the water was not fit for swimming. The quality of water has improved in recent years but is still not fit for swimming. Our friend dove into the lake from the grassy bank and came up gasping; the stench was too much! She lost no time in scrambling up the bank and racing uphill to the house.

However, the lake was good for boating. It became clear to Robert and me that the canoe was not the best mode of transportation on the river if we wanted to do any serious fishing or wanted to take more than two people. We needed to expand our fleet. At that time there were no sales outlets for boats in the Woodstock area, except for the Sears Canada Inc. catalogue store. We were brought up on catalogue shopping and still buy many products this way. We poured through the pages of the latest Sears offering and decided on a 12-foot sportsman's runabout and a small outboard motor. When it arrived we were impressed with the fiberglass construction, the wet well, and the sleek lines of the boat. It proved to be just what was needed, including a set of sturdy oars in case of outboard failure, a common occurrence as any sportsman will testify.

The runabout made it possible to take more people for a spin on the river, more safely. The small outboard was tested to its limit at times when the boat was headed into a stiff breeze but the runabout had her sea legs and handled well in rough waters. It was also a superior craft for fishing. Find the right spot, drop the anchor, and fish away to your heart's content. What every fisherman knows, and few non-anglers realize, is that catching fish is not all that important, not the ultimate goal. Fishing is the art of getting away from the stress of everyday living, of relaxing, wiping the mind free of cares and woes, the fellowship involved in being with a good friend. Anglers can have a joyful day even if they land no fish. Good thing, too! There's not much to catch in Mactaquac Lake near the farm.

Robert and I gave up fishing in the river at Twin Pines Farm long ago, though Marshall and Doug have spent many happy hours with rod and reel, trying their luck from a perch on the rocks or from canoe or boat. Most of their catches wound up as feed for their hens and chickens, though several good size bass have been caught.

This is not to say that Mactaquac Lake is not productive when it comes to fishing. The opposite is true. This 65-mile body of water has become one of the finest sources of bass in North America, the site for an annual tournament that draws competitors from the

United States and many parts of Canada. Perhaps this great population of bass will some day expand its territory to include the area off Twin Pines Farm. Meanwhile, good bass fishing exists from Woodstock to the Mactaquac Dam and many participate in the sport.

It's too bad that the lake is so underdeveloped. It has the potential to be a major attraction for tourists and to serve New Brunswickers. It is amazing that New Brunswick's great network of lakes, rivers and streams, plus the thousands of miles of saltwater coast, have never been developed to their potential. There is limited development, some excellent marinas on the east coast, in the Saint John area, and at Mactaquac Park above Fredericton. There are plans for waterfront development and marinas at both Fredericton and Woodstock.

Private enterprise has done little to encourage boating as a recreation and the provincial government has done even less, with the exception, perhaps, of the excellent facilities at Mactaquac Provincial Park. It is beyond comprehension that a huge 65-mile long lake, nestled in a beautiful wooded valley, would not have a string of marinas, boatyards, motels, restaurants, camping facilities and rest areas. You see more snowmobiles on the head pond during the winter months than you do sailboats, power cruisers, runabouts and canoes in summer. Boating should be promoted in New Brunswick, both by the government and by private entrepreneurs!

That's part of an ongoing dream. I am satisfied with my canoe and green runabout; they meet my needs at this time, but I'd like to have a bigger power boat, with bunks and a galley, that could be used for overnight cruises. It would be wonderful to load a party aboard the cruiser at Twin Pines, travel downriver to Mactaquac, portage around the dam and continue to Fredericton for a visit, then up the Jemseg to Grand Lake, back to the St. John and down to the Port City. From there the possibilities are limitless: a grand cruise of the Bay of Fundy, stopping in at communities in New Brunswick and Nova Scotia; a cruise down the east coast, from Maine to Florida. Nor do we have to leave the St. John River for exciting adventure.

A trip from the farm could be upriver, to Hartland, Bristol, Bath, to the Beechwood Dam, then a portage and continue up river to

Perth-Andover and to the grand spectacle of Grand Falls. Another portage and we could travel to Edmundston. A spectacular side trip could be made with a portage at the Tobique Dam and a cruise up the Tobique head pond to Plaster Rock.

One day Kay and I will sit in our chairs on the deck of our home at Twin Pines and watch with wonder as sailboats and cruisers pass before our eyes on the mighty St. John, another dream fulfilled.

17

Fighting Old Man Winter

The wind howled from the North as it swept across half a mile of open fields; the television antenna attached to the house at Twin Pines Farm sent shock waves through the building as it fought the gale. An eerie keening echoed through the house as the wind plucked the arms of the antenna. Kay heard a strange sound from the direction of the huge picture window that gives a view of the St. John River and the deck outside. As she looked in the direction of the window she could see the glass bowing in gentle undulations as the wind tried to pluck it from its frame. The outside thermometer read a brisk twenty-five degrees below zero. It wasn't a typical winter day at the farm. Neither was it an uncommon one, weather wise.

As I gazed out the kitchen window to check the condition of the steep driveway the gale-driven snow swirled in an opaque white sheet. It was impossible to see the two towering pines just fifty feet away.

"I guess we won't be going to work this morning, not until this clears up a bit," I said to Kay resignedly. "I've no idea if the driveway is filled with snow."

It was, of course. This is a common occurrence at Twin Pines Farm when Old Man Winter really takes over, usually in January and February but no rarity earlier in the season. We had known from the time we bought the property that we would have some tough days when the driveway would be impassable because of drifting snow. We had intentionally built the house some distance down in the field from Route 103 to assure that no one could build too near us, so we could enjoy space. There would be days when it would be impossible to get a vehicle up or down the gravel driveway. We didn't realize, however, just how strong the winds would be and how high and solid the snow drifts could become.

The first winter we spent at Twin Pines, Bruce tried to keep the driveway open with our garden tractor and attached snow blower. That didn't last long. The spiral of the blower was soon completely twisted and snarled from trying to accommodate large rocks from the driveway. Next a local farmer tried the chore with his large tractor, also equipped with a snow blower. It did a much better job, the blower digesting the snow and rocks and blasting them thirty feet into the fields on either side of the driveway. Now we could get cars up and down with no trouble. Unfortunately, increased insurance rates made it impractical for our neighbour to continue his snow plowing operations and we were back to square one, forcing us to look for another solution.

We were late for work on a number of occasions during those early years because of a snow-packed driveway, cars trapped in the yard. Looking back I can see that we were lucky to some degree. It could have been worse. The St. John River Valley is notorious for its high winds as they roar down from the North. This is farm country and often there is a lot of open and acres of bare fields between homes. Sections of Route 103 between Upper Woodstock and Victoria Corner are subject to drifting that often makes passage impossible until the government plows have done their job. One particularly bad section parallels the road frontage at Twin Pines. There have been days when you could shovel and scrape and get your car to the road, only to find the highway blocked by high drifts.

We thought we had the problem almost solved when we decided to erect a two car garage near the highway, between the two arms of our upper driveway. We would be able to keep our vehicles out of the weather and it shouldn't be too tough a task to clear snow from the garage to Route 103, a matter of only thirty feet or so. Having decided that my country-carpenter skills were not up to such a major project, including pouring cement for a solid pad for the garage, I called upon neighbour Bob McLaughlin for professional help. Bob is founder and owner of McLaughlin Roof Trusses Ltd., famous throughout the province for the high quality of his prefab trusses and small buildings.

It was not difficult to get in touch with Bob; his home and his ever-expanding woodworking plant are located only a stone's throw from Twin Pines. He would be glad to contract the job, he said, and his price seemed most reasonable. I explained why I wanted the garage and indicated the spot I would prefer to have it located. No problem. Bob was as good as his word. Soon the cement truck arrived, the pad was poured, the building frame in place and metal roof and sides attached. Two steel doors completed the job. Now our cars would be sheltered from wind, snow, sleet and rain, and any other surprises Old Man Winter might throw our way. Surely it wouldn't be too hard to shovel a path to Route 103. Time proved we were too optimistic but the garage has served us well.

The next problem to tackle was that of drifting snow blocking the way down to the house. The driveway runs east-west for most of its length and the prevailing north wind doesn't take long to fill it with snow. We discovered that on bad days the driveway would fill with snow only hours after it had been plowed. It was essential to keep it open in case of a fire or some other emergency. Why not erect a snow fence, a friend suggested. Good idea. I was familiar with this strategy to prevent drifting. I'd even witnessed the wood-slatted fencing being made in Lakeville many years ago, though that plant was no longer operating.

After asking a lot of questions and chasing up a few blind alleys, I found the snow fence I required in a local hardware store in Woodstock. Robert, Marshall and Doug helped erect it the first winter we tried this approach. Posts were pounded into the field adjacent to the northern side of the driveway and the fencing attached. It worked to a degree but there was still considerable drifting at times. It was then suggested that the fence had been placed too close to the driveway to be fully effective. It should run parallel but be erected at a distance of fifty feet or so. Now we've got the right formula and the snow fence does work — when properly erected. A couple of times we were late erecting it and, unable to pound the posts into the frozen earth, had to compromise. Though braces were used they were no match for winter winds and the snow fence fell over on these occasions.

We'll probably never completely solve the problem of a snow-filled driveway. The snow fence helps. The garage has proved to be a lifesaver. Once the snow starts to come in quantity the cars are kept uphill in the garage. This often means an uncomfortable walk up the driveway if the plow hasn't yet appeared to clear the way, the two of us floundering through waist-high snow to reach the garage. However, now that we've at least semi-retired there is seldom an occasion when we have to be in town at a specific time.

As you get older it seems that winters are longer, colder and there's more snow. It's not true, of course. There were snow storms when I was a boy that created drifts almost as high as the telephone poles, or so it seemed. The poles were shorter then and perhaps memory magnifies the intensity of the storms and the height of the snow. Still, I know that the winters of the 1980s were no more severe than those when I walked a mile to the one room school at Avondale, bundled up so tightly I could hardly put one foot ahead of the other. Nor are winters any colder than they were in decades past; it just seems that way.

That's not to say that New Brunswick winters are not a challenge to man and beast. They are. If you live in a home built in the middle of a vast open space you can't get by with a potbellied Quebec heater and no insulation in the walls. When we built at Twin Pines we thought we had protected ourselves against Old Man Winter with adequate insulation, no doors or windows in the exposed north side of the building, electric heat in every room with separate thermostats, a brick fireplace in the living room and a built-in Franklin-type iron fireplace in the office-library-den downstairs. We should be snug and cozy, ready for anything winter could throw at us. We were, almost. We soon discovered what every homeowner should know: fireplaces suck the heat out of a house at an alarming rate, almost as fast as heating systems can produce it.

This discovery led to a number of trials and errors before the right combination was found. Our first attempt was to get a set of black iron-bound tempered-glass folding doors for the upstairs fireplace. The doors could be left open while a fire was burning, or be closed. We chose the latter because it helped prevent the heat of the house from being drawn up the chimney. A cover over the front of the seldom-used Franklin solved the problem in that room. These improvements made it feel as if the house was warmer but you couldn't prove it when you perused the monthly bill from NB Power. It was high!

There was some relief when we ran into trouble with the outside deck which had rotted because of the greenhouse we had attached. The same contractor who designed and built a solid new deck also took the siding off the house and applied sheet insulation to the exterior. Now we had insulation in the walls, on the exterior of the house under the siding, and an extra layer added in the attic ceiling. Windows and doors were recaulked and we were well prepared for another cold winter.

The next step was to improve the heating system, if we could, to cut that expense. We were thinking of retirement days when pension cheques might not cover as many bills as does the income when you are working. Why not try a fireplace-insert, a new weapon against the penetrating cold of our winters?

We read as many articles as we could find on the pros and cons of inserts, some praising them for their heating qualities and energy saving, others warning of possible hazards. The consensus seemed to be that they saved money in energy costs and added comfort to the home. We visited a number of homes that had taken this route and came away with a favorable impression. There are a number of units available from several companies and it is not difficult to find them. Costs vary, as does quality. We were advised that we should settle for nothing less than an air-tight insert and it should be custom-fitted to our fireplace. We were also cautioned that we should have the chimney cleaned each year to avoid super-heated flue fires that would endanger the house.

We finally found the insert we thought would be adequate to our needs and had it installed. It was one of the best investments we have ever made. We both love the warmth provided by burning wood; it seems to be more comfortable than that given by electric heaters, oil or gas furnaces. It compares most favorably with baseboard hot water systems we've enjoyed in a few of our homes over the years. We've been delighted with our fireplace-insert and get by with three cords of hardwood per winter. We seldom turn on our electric heating system, except in the late fall and late spring when the fireplace would give too much steady heat.

Heating and insulation can assure comfort inside the home but it would be impossible to completely defend against winter. Mother Nature has tricks she hasn't even tried yet. One of her nastiest, an annual irritant, is ice on the driveway making it impossible for any vehicle to get up to the road and a real hazard for any trying to get down to the house. Months of plowing, vehicles packing snow into a solid mass, create just the right conditions for a glacier of ice once a thaw arrives. Torrents of water cascade down the driveway and create a miniature lake in the yard in front of the house, a lake contained by an almost complete circle of high banks of snow packed there by a series of plowing operations. At those times even the short trip from the garage to the main road becomes an unforgettable adventure. The winter of 1988-89 was the worst in our memory for ice on the driveway and was the first time we have ever had to have it salted and sanded, an expensive operation.

There are positive things to say about winter, of course. When we first moved to Twin Pines we could hardly wait for winter to arrive and the anticipated adventure of snowshoeing through our woods, up and down hill, seeking evidence of wildlife. The snowshoes haven't been used for years. The toboggan and sled are used to transport groceries from the garage to the house. Kay and I no longer enjoy those sports and the grandchildren living closest to us have graduated to more modern sports, such as snowmobiling.

I have a prejudice against snowmobiles, considering them to be noisy, smelly machines, evil in nature. That's a subjective reaction, I realize. Some of my best friends are snowmobilers. My one and only adventure on one of these frenzied machines ended just as I suspected it would, with me face first in the snow. We had gone to the MacFarlane house, just across the south field, for dinner and had left some essential ingredient at home. No problem, said grandson Marshall, I'll run you down on my snowmobile. I objected strenuously. No, no, he said, it won't take us long and the snow's too heavy for walking. I bundled up warmly and left the house, climbing onto the snorting, bellowing, stinking monster with great reluctance.

"Here we go," Marshall bellowed over the roar of the machine as I gave him a bear hug that must have bruised his ribs. And away we went, zooming across the field, leaving a rooster tail of billowing snow in our wake. It happened when Marshall took a sharp starboard turn to head down to the house at Twin Pines. Suddenly I was airborne, arms and legs flailing, before my face was buried in the deep snow. I struggled to my feet, shaking my fist at the back of the disappearing snowmobile. Marshall didn't even miss me, though he must have wondered why I had released my frantic bear hug. I plowed my way through the deep snow of the field to the driveway and struggled down to the house, digging snow from around my neck.

When I arrived in the yard and Marshall saw my bedraggled condition, my red, snow-scrubbed face, he laughed so hard he couldn't talk. After getting what we had come for and locking the door, Marshall invited me to climb aboard his wicked machine.

"Thank you, no," I said stiffly. "I believe I'll walk."

The most enjoyable part of winters is the panoramic view from Twin Pines. It is spectacular after the snow has arrived to stay for a few months, particularly after one of those wet snow storms when the bare limbs of hardwoods take on a coat of white, and evergreens appear even more majestic than usual as if wearing expensive ermine coats. There's no season when the scenery at Twin Pines is not breathtaking.

18
"There Are None So Blind . . . "

Being a klutz is no excuse for being blind to the wonders of nature. It may be quoting American authoress Gertrude Atherton out of context but her words still apply: "The very commonplaces of life are components of its eternal mystery." Anyone who lives in the country should be aware of the tremendous variety of wildlife in evidence: birds, animals, bugs and insects, reptiles, aquatic life; in the air, in the trees, on the ground, beneath the soil, and in water — springs, ponds, lakes and rivers. This magic world is there to observe in all four seasons if you but open your eyes and absorb what is happening. This is also true for those who live in villages, towns and cities, though the variety of wildlife is not so rich in urban areas.

In the words of English novelist Charles Dickens: "Nature gives to every time and season some beauties of its own; and from morning to night, as from the cradle to the grave, is but a succession of changes so gentle and easy that we can scarcely mark their progress."

The changes may be "gentle and easy" but nature is relentless in her fight to create the environment in her own image.

Those who wish to be informed watchers of nature should arm themselves with notebook and pencil, binoculars and specific guide-books. And a camera. In New Brunswick a "must" book is *The Birds of New Brunswick* by W. Austin Squires.

Kay and I have always been birdwatchers, though not in the dedicated sense of organized clubs, field trips, study and debate. We just enjoy watching birds. There's no shortage of our wild feathered friends at Twin Pines Farm, regardless of the season. We have observed many different species, from the raptorial, to the aquatic, to songbirds, to crows and ravens. We have done so most often without having to leave the deck of the house; we have expanded our list of sightings by walks in the woods at Twin Pines and by visits to the shoreline when lured by the eerie cry of the loon. We keep no formal record of our sightings, though we can tell you what birds stay at the farm during the winter, the first to be expected in the spring, the last to leave in the fall. Our five bird guidebooks are well worn through years of use. We are not experts, not naturalists in the true sense, but we are informed observers.

Nature neglects no season in providing birds and animals to be seen and admired. The approach of winter may drive away many of our summer visitors but it also attracts other birds to our home. By late September or early October the noisy blue jays have already started to appear at our deck, complaining vigorously when they discover we have not yet erected our bird feeders. They have returned to their homes in the woods by the time the Red-winged Blackbirds arrive in the spring.

We started erecting bird feeders in the 1960s when we lived in Connecticut and were surprised when beautiful red cardinals appeared and stayed with us during the winter, as did sleek mourning doves. We have seen neither of these two birds at our feeders at the farm. We do have four pairs of blue jays each winter, a large flock of evening grosbeaks and four pair of black-capped chickadees (the official bird of New Brunswick). These are the regulars. Infrequent visitors at the feeders include redpolls, purple and pine siskins, juncos, downy and hairy woodpeckers. Sparrows do make an appearance but don't seem to be able to cope with sunflower seeds, the only food we supply. We are happy with our regular clients, eating only a few feet from us and clearly observed through the picture window and glass patio doors. Another occasional visitor is a red squirrel; a favorite photo is one I took of the squirrel sharing the elevated feeder with a black-capped chickadee. Close up photography is easy from the comfort of the living room at Twin Pines as the feeders are attached to the deck rail, only eight feet away. Two feeders, attached to the picture window by suction cups, allow even more intimate photo opportunities.

Hawks — red-tailed, swamp and sparrow — are not uncommon at Twin Pines, particularly during the warmer months. Other visiting raptors at the farm include a bald eagle, osprey, and owls, including the darlings of the family, a pair of saw-whet, and a rare (for us) sighting of a snowy owl.

There is evidence that the red-tailed hawk hangs around the woods at the farm during the winter months. It can be seen gliding low over the fields looking for dinner, and we came across a rabbit kill that painted the snow red and left wing and talon tracks as mute testimony. These hawks are seldom seen in the open spaces when there is a heavy snow cover but appear when wind and sun have combined to create oases of brown grass in the fields and mice are more easily detected.

We are grateful that the sparrow hawk (American kestrel) does not winter at Twin Pines, though this tiny falcon is a perennial summer visitor. We saw how effective this feathered killing machine can be when we had a feeder in Connecticut. As we watched from our window a sparrow hawk streaked into view, snatched a sparrow and was gone in an instant. It was not a pretty sight but we couldn't help but admire the hawk for its speed and skill in hunting. The sparrow hawk is amazing in its ability to hover for minutes, seemingly motionless, as it looks for prey.

We never tire of our winter visitors. They provide live entertainment and wonderment every day. The first diners to arrive at the feeders in the morning are the black-capped chickadees, and they are the last to leave. Then comes an advance patrol of evening grosbeaks, followed soon after by a flock of thirty or more of their brothers and sisters, parents, uncles, aunts, and friends. Juncos arrive about the same time. The blue jays are usually the sleepy heads, waiting until the chickadees, juncos and grosbeaks have had a chance at the feeders.

The birds put on quite a show for the price of a few sunflower seeds. The chickadees dart to a feeder, grab a seed and usually return immediately to the nearby old apple tree. Occasionally a chickadee will grab a seed, hold it by both feet against the edge of the wooden rail of the feeder and peck at it vigorously until it gets the meat. Blue jays, in a hurry for a quick fix, will also employ this method of getting the meat of the seed. Grosbeaks tend to be bullies, the dogs-in-the-manger of the bird world, imposing a territorial claim to the feeder and chasing away other hungry birds until he or she meets the same fate. They depart when the blue jays arrive. Not the chickadee, a fearless little bird. They will dart at the feeder even when it is guarded by grosbeaks or blue jays, and will share seeds with a squirrel. They are all delightful winter companions who disappear once the snow is gone and the influx of summer residents starts. They can still be seen and enjoyed if you visit the nearby woods where they nest.

Many people judge the arrival of spring by the appearance of the first American Robin, their red breasts a sign of season change. They are not always the harbinger of spring at the farm, as often a pair of transient ducks will be the first arrivals and will settle on the pond for a snack and short rest. Red-winged blackbirds always make a home at Twin Pines, usually quite a few pairs, sometimes appearing before the robins arrive.

When the in-migration has been completed the air at Twin Pines Farm is filled with the harmonic sound of a variety of birds singing their individual songs, sometimes courting, chickadee often challenging, and regularly voicing territorial imperative. Some of the summer residents seem to appear in flocks, such as the bobolink with its distinctive buff cap. This is a meadowland bird that will prepare its nest in a hay field or stand of grain before there is much growth, remaining there until the family is grown and ready to leave. They fill the air with music as they sway atop a thin straw of hay or grain. It is uncanny, a never explained mystery, how the bobolink seems to know to the day when the mowing machine will appear to cut the hay. The bobolinks will invariably take off the day before the mower arrives.

Another favorite at Twin Pines Farm is the killdeer, a member of the plover family that also nests in our meadows when it arrives. It is not an annual visitor to the farm but creates a lot of joy when it does.

A rare visitor to Twin Pines and to New Brunswick is the mockingbird, one of the Mimidae family found as a permanent resident throughout most of the United Sates, Mexico and the West Indies. One morning while Kay was working in the house she was impressed with the volume and singing of a bird outside. Later she heard another song, different from the first, then another. This singing kept up for several hours but it seemed to come from different birds. Her curiosity piqued, Kay grabbed one of our bird guidebooks, the binoculars and started a search. She found the bird sitting atop the tall pine in the yard, singing its heart out. It was a mockingbird! If it has ever appeared at the farm since that one sighting, no one has reported it to us.

Birdwatchers can enjoy themselves at the farm during all four seasons. Other birds we have sighted, some of them residents during specific seasons are: black ducks, mallards, blue heron (the rascal that cleaned the brook trout out of our pond), kingfisher, shrike, pine grosbeak, rose-breasted grosbeak, phoebe, kingbird, red poll, purple and gold finches, baltimore oriole, grackle, starling, cowbird, warbler, ring-necked pheasant, Canada goose, junco, sparrows (many varieties), swallows (English, barn and tree), cedar waxwings and purple martins. We have sighted others at the farm, sometimes in the woods, often in trees close to the house, but we have not been able to identify them because of their brief stay or because they were in flight.

We have tried to get the purple martins to make Twin Pines their annual summer home but, as of this writing, our attempts have met with failure, despite the fact that we have erected a modern, twelve room apartment house for their use. One year we did have purple martins arrive and look over the inviting apartment house. A female started to harvest straws from the rock garden for a nest but was discouraged by a male and eventually they flew away. There are other birds more than willing to occupy the fine bird house, especially sparrows, but for the last few years it has been inhabited by tree swallows. These beautiful birds with high-tech streamlined bodies are almost as good as purple martins at reducing the population of mosquitoes and other stinging insects.

Birds are not the only wildlife attraction at Twin Pines Farm. There are snakes and a variety of furred animals. Kay has a strange, to me, empathy with snakes. I don't. She was the first to discover we had at least one family of reptiles on the property, a meter long specimen sunning itself on a straw pile near the barn. Grandson Doug, then but a lad, promptly named it "Ralph," a name that has been passed on to all snakes at the farm ever since. We haven't identified the type of snake this might be but it seems to be harmless. No one has been attacked or even threatened. Snakes shed their skins as they grow and finding these abandoned skins has become an annual treasure hunt at Twin Pines.

Wild animals that have made a home at Twin Pines include: raccoons, rabbits, groundhogs, porcupines, skunks, weasels, muskrats, squirrels (grey, red and flying), several types of mice, and a fox. Regular visitors, not believed to be permanent residents, include moose and deer. We suspect we have had sightings of coyotes but couldn't get a long enough observation to be sure.

When you are living in the country you must keep your eyes open at all times, and your ears cocked for unusual sounds, if you want to enjoy a glimpse of wild animals. Most of them are quite shy of humans, with the exception of skunks, porcupines and groundhogs.

One day I was resting in my favorite chair in the living room and reading a book when I heard a commotion outside. I went to the glass patio doors and looked in the direction of the distraction and saw two moose standing in the pond, plunging their heads into the water and coming up with a mouth full of dripping aquatic plants. I eased out the door and to the north of the deck, calling softly to Kay to come and look. She left the garden and just as she was coming onto the deck a third moose shouldered its way through the alders and willows and joined the other two in the water. We watched for several minutes, the animals looking in our direction occasionally and deciding we were no threat. When they had satisfied their thirst and their need for food, they climbed out of the pond and meandered across the meadow without a backward glance.

Another time when Beth and family were visiting, helping with the work to be done in the garden, young Doug wandered away, as boys are predestined to do. When Beth went to search for him she saw Doug standing about half way up the gravel driveway confronting a large moose that appeared to be on its way down. The lad showed no fear of the beast.

There have been numerous sightings of moose and deer over the years but we have no evidence they stay on the farm for anything more than a visit. We see too much of groundhogs during the summer and their populations can explode alarmingly. Raccoons are nocturnal and seldom come near the house but most years they will do a real job on a patch of corn. These lovable black-masked bandits know when the corn is ripe and have no compunction about stealing every last ear.

One year, weary of having the raccoons getting to the corn before we had an opportunity, we asked grandson Marshall to catch the marauders in a live trap, transport them to some other location and set them free. We were away for a few days and when we came back and entered the kitchen we were almost overcome by the strong scent of skunk perfume. It turned out that Marshall the Trapper had had a successful battle against the garden bandits, had caught a number of raccoons and then released them. One morning when he went to check his live traps, he had a black visitor inside, one with a broad white stripe down its back.

The skunk was not amused! Though Marshall avoided being hit by a direct shot from the skunk's weaponry, he did manage to pick up considerable perfume on his clothes. It was when he went into the house to wash his hands that he left enough of the scent to greet Kay and me when we arrived home.

Twin Pines has its own resident fox family. We presume it's a family though we have never seen more than one animal at a time. One day our dog, Lady Mae, was making a terrible commotion, standing at the north end of the deck, looking towards the barn, and barking excitedly. Suddenly she took off in high gear. Lady Mae often sounded false alarms, probably because she was scared of her own shadow, but most often it was because she had seen something unusual, an intruder on her territorial turf. I ran out onto the deck, wondering if we were being visited by a moose or a deer. Looking in the direction of the barn I could see Lady Mae standing firmly on her four legs, her head lowered in a threatening manner, hairs on her neck erect, voicing warning growls. Not twenty-five feet away, facing the dog, a red fox had assumed a similar position. I feared for Lady Mae. The two were about the same size but I knew the fox had more courage and a greater ability to fight. Still, it was impossible to keep from grinning: they looked like two gunfighters staring each other down, both afraid to make the first move to a showdown. I called Lady Mae several times before she gave up her fighting pose and returned to the deck. The fox turned and left.

That red fox is no stranger to Twin Pines. We call him Foxy Freddy, after the character in two children's books. We believe we have found his burrow deep in the woods but close to the river. We've never tried to find out for sure, afraid we might do something that would convince him he should move to some other territory. We like having him around. Foxy Freddy puts on quite a show during the winter months, when snow covers the meadows and pastures. We see him often then, snuffling his way through the meadow, searching for a meal of mice. Suddenly he will stop, jump into the air as if he had springs on all four feet, and then pounce for his prey. If Lady Mae spotted Freddy stalking the fields before we did, she would give her excited bark. Yet when allowed out onto the deck she would usually just sit and watch Freddy at work. Perhaps the dog learned a trick or two. One day I was walking through the upper field with Lady Mae before snow covered the ground and she was acting just like the fox, sniffing the ground, snuffling at holes. Suddenly she pounced and came up with a mouse.

There's more than birds and animals to observe at Twin Pines Farm. Flowers appear in the woods before all of the snow is gone and new varieties come along from week to week. The meadows and pastures change from dull brown to rich green, flowers of many colors and hues painting highlights in the verdant blanket, from spring to fall.

At Twin Pines Farm, as elsewhere, one must use all of the senses to truly appreciate the full beneficence of nature. Sight and sound are vital to understanding. However, to extend an old axiom: There are none so blind as those who will not see . . . or hear, or smell, or taste or touch. We are in touch with nature at Twin Pines when we breathe in the earthy aroma of fiddleheads as they are picked each spring, the heady perfume of apple trees in blossom, the smell of sweet grass and clover; experience the joy of biting into wild strawberries and a few weeks later wild raspberries, perennial treats for the taste buds; sense the comforting feel of soft, furry pussywillows as they herald the arrival of spring; are reborn as hands dig into the moist earth during planting time, the texture and the aroma awakening a familiar sense of oneness with nature. This is a magic world!

19
Nature Fights Back

Nature never gives up the fight to control her environment, despite the efforts of man to make changes. Tiny, delicate blades of grass penetrate cracks in cement or asphalt as nature commences regeneration; clear-cut forests will soon be green again, an orderly process that starts with cover crops and only decades later will see mature stands of hardwood trees or evergreens; fields and meadows, artificially imposed by mankind, are restored to a standard and quality not dictated by man.

It took countless centuries for nature to develop the mixed forest that covered the land now occupied by Twin Pines Farm. It was still a forest back in the 1800s, a mixture of hardwoods and softwoods that stretched back for miles from the (then) quick flowing waters of the St. John River. Malecites paddled their canoes up and down this familiar valley river, picking fiddleheads along the bank, harvesting bark from huge white birches to build canoes, spearing salmon for food, hunting deer and moose and game birds. These First Canadians lived and worked with nature, not against her, and all was well in this idyllic period.

Then came the settlers, the land grants, and the stripping of forests to prepare the earth for planting, the use of logs for construction of homes and other buildings. There was then, as there is today, a tremendous waste of nature's produce, always a price paid when clear-cutting methods are used. There was less waste by those early settlers than is the case today. Trees were felled to clear the land, to make lumber for shelter, and to be used as fuel during long, harsh winters. Fires fed by brush and branches added nutrients to the relatively thin soil. Stumps were uprooted and torn from the earth to create fields for crops and pasturing livestock.

Slowly but surely the land was tamed, no easy task in Carleton County where rocks are a constant threat to ploughs and other machinery. A cultivated piece of ground can be cleared of stones but other rocks take their place within a year. Nature never gives up the battle to reclaim her rightful land, to reimpose proper stewardship. She is relentless in trying to restore a grand design not appreciated nor tolerated by man. There has been no slackening in this struggle since the destruction of the primal forest at Twin Pines in the 1800s. Successive "owners" have made their own adjustments to the land, changing pastures, planting different crops, shifting rock fences in contour, livestock having engraved deep trails in the earth through decades of use.

The task of clearing land is a tough one, easier today than when much of the work had to be done by brute strength, man and beast, without the benefit of motorized machinery. There has to be grudging admiration for those early farmers who not only cultivated the land, tamed it to their needs and desires, but also had to conduct an ongoing fight against a determined nature.

At Twin Pines Farm we reached an accommodation with nature. A temporary victory in halting the advance of alders up the hill convinced us that we were wrong, that nature is a better landscape artist than we are, that her grand design has purpose. Red willows, that seem to have taken over abandoned fields all over the county, have made their appearance at Twin Pines. Sumac — favored by many home-owners as an ornamental — is spreading rapidly. Nature uses alders, sumacs, willows and other weed trees and shrubs as a conservation tool to fight erosion. She is relentless in pursuit of her own design for this piece of valley hillside, a haven for animals and birds, with a mixture of hardwoods, softwoods, wildflowers and grasses.

A grove of poplars, whispering sentinels on a windy day, has created a border at the lower end of the north field. A lone poplar stands guard at the south end of the pond, looking lonely against the background of a thick cluster of sumacs only ten feet away. It is fascinating to witness nature at work, slowly but surely transforming the appearance of woods and fields.

The battle for the ponds is far from over. Though silt carried by the small feeder stream has filled in part of the upper pond and aquatic grass and bulrushes have taken root, remedial action will be taken. The water area of the first pond has shrunk each year as the gentle brook gurgles more slowly down the slope and vegetation claims more of the pond.

Temporary abdication of stewardship on the part of the owner was not a voluntary move. A car accident a few years ago took its toll: a back injury that ruled out practically any physical effort necessary to wage the continual struggle against a determined nature. Now, with retirement, there is time to plan and execute improvements to the farm, including both ponds. Nature will be allowed to make some progress but we will decide the where, if not the when.

When cultivation ceases, nature is quick to fill the void. Her grand design may be marked by a spurt in the population of weed trees, such as alders and the staghorn sumac, an easy task when these are already present on the property. Beaked hazelnuts become more common, as may mountain maple and one or more of the twenty-eight varieties of willows found in New Brunswick; wild raspberry patches spread quickly in the former pastures and meadows; choke cherry bushes expand their territory; firs and spruce nose up through the earth, sheltered in their infancy by the weed trees.

A good description of the types of weed trees and shrubs nature uses in reclaiming territory is found in *Weeds of the Woods: Some Small Trees and Shrubs of New Brunswick* by Glen Blouin.

Nature has her own work force. Birds not only broadcast seeds from trees, shrubs and flowers found at Twin Pines Farm, they bring in different varieties from other areas. Squirrels play an important role in "planting" seeds from trees, such as hazelnut and butternut. Droppings from birds and animals are used by nature to regenerate pastures and meadows into woods and, eventually, forests.

There's nothing drab about nature's grand design. She is prolific with beautiful wildflowers and colorful weeds. She works with a rich palette to produce kaleidoscopic results. One person's weed is another's wildflower: the graceful, if spiny, Scotch thistle is a weed when its pink or purple flower rears above the grain or timothy in a field, but it is a magnificent wildflower when it appears in an abandoned pasture or meadow. The first wildflowers of the year at Twin Pines Farm are trilliums and violets (yellow and blue). They are found in the woods and expand their territory, as nature slowly but surely reclaims more land as we push ahead with other plans, pleased that we are working in partnership with a brilliant landscape artist.

The bane of most homeowners is the prolific yellow dandelion as it takes over lawns all over North America. Yet this beautiful wildflower is a sight to behold when it fills entire fields. It is a useful weed because its leaves make a fine green for eating, while its yellow flower makes an excellent home wine.

Clovers, white and purple, are a wildflower but can also be a valuable forage crop. They produce honey and attract both domestic bees and the larger bumblebee. Other wildflowers found during walks at Twin Pines Farm include: mallows, in a variety of colors; fireweeds, pink or lavender; milkweed, tall and stout of stem, noted for their parachute seeds widely distributed by early fall winds; asters, also popular in many flower gardens; vetches, their pea-like flowers usually blue or purple at Twin Pines; bellflowers, so called because of their delicate bell-shaped bluish flowers; and chicory, with light blue flowers, whose root can be roasted and used as a coffee substitute.

There are more than 150 native North American species of lupines but only one is common in the northeast. These beautiful finger-leaved plants are found in great number along New Brunswick's roads and highways, as well as in fields that have been abandoned. They are popular in flower gardens. Lupines are not popular with farmers as the plants are poisonous to cattle. Coneflowers are no strangers to Twin Pines, particularly the lovely black-eyed Susan. It may be a weed in a field of grain but it is widely cultivated by flower gardeners. The golden petals of the black-eyed Susan can be plucked in that ageless love game of "She loves me, she loves me not . . . "

Another wildflower used in romantic games is the prolific buttercup. There's little romantic about the appearance of goldenrod at Twin Pines Farm, or elsewhere, as it is often blamed for the annual epidemic of hay fever in the fall. This may be a bum rap; ragweeds often cause more suffering for pollen-sensitive people. Sticktights, with a beautiful yellow ray flower, may not cause hayfever but they can cause discomfort as their pronged seeds attach to clothing or to skin. Other yellow wildflowers at Twin Pines Farm include: adder-tongues, yellow, violet or white, with mottled leaves; mulleins, a stout plant with five-petaled yellow flowers; the ever popular butter-and-eggs; and the golden-eyed white daisy, a near relative of cultivated chrysanthemums.

When strolling across, up and down the acres of Twin Pines, depending on the time of the year, you're likely to see saxifrages with clusters of tiny white flowers; or the bunchberry, with pretty white flowers and, later in the year, bunches of red berries; the prolific common chickweed, with deeply notched white petals, will be an ongoing problem for gardeners earlier in the year; while the bedstraw (an herb) may be missed by the unobservant eye because it is small and delicate.

Nature uses all of the tools at her disposal when she sets out to reclaim a piece of land that has been cultivated. There is a pattern to her reconstruction work, a combination of trees, shrubs, wild-flowers, weeds, mosses and grasses as the soil is regenerated for future use as open woods and forest.

The battle continues at Twin Pines Farm with nature being allowed to reclaim land from projects we have abandoned. Her work has to be seen to be appreciated. Our covenant with her is that we will pursue our dreams and she can carry on with her restoration work over much of the farm.

20
A Dream Realized

"So I have nothing? Ah, you're wrong. Why, I have all my dreams
— priceless are my riches when my brain with fancy teems."
Dorothy Snowden

There are dreams and there are dreams. Those we have while sleeping should not be confused with those we have when we're awake. Those we have while sleeping may be good, bad or unexplainable. Some are nightmares. Those we have while awake can be real, and be realized, if we but pursue them with diligence and, often, sacrifice. Some of these can be nightmares, too.

Kay and I had a long-time dream of finding a place in the country where we could build a home and settle down to a life less hectic than that of the city. We like space around us. We enjoy the outdoor life, quiet walks through the woods seeking out flowers and trees, animals and birds, a paddle on the river, the challenge of a vegetable garden, a flower bed, sometimes a barbecue.

It took four decades before we attained our dream, a place in the country, free of mortgage, an oasis of contentment for our senior years. Dreams are seldom fulfilled entirely; compromises must be made, often goals must be adapted to meet the demands of reality. Perhaps in dreaming we often aim too high and must settle for less. If so, that does nothing to diminish the pleasure enjoyed when a dream is realized.

There have been many changes in our dream, none of them sufficient to tarnish the luster of achievement. The very name of the place, Twin Pines Farm, had to be changed to Lone Pine Farm when one of our sturdy trees was stricken with disease and a chain saw brought it to earth. Now it is Lone Pine Farm. Soon the name will again change, to The Pines, thanks to a large number of seedlings planted by grandson Marshall. We will have a fine grove of red pines, as well as a border of them along our cedar rail fence.

The house itself is a far cry from the one we had envisioned in our dreams. We planned to erect a log home, one with larger rooms and more space than the one we have. Yet, we wouldn't trade our house for the finest log home in the land. We feel we have realized our favorite dream: a home in the country, in a beautiful valley with a river bordering the property, and plenty of space to carry out projects not yet completed.

The ponds have given us much pleasure and continue to do so. Much work remains to be done but one day there will again be trout swimming around and being fed by hand. There are few walking or riding trails through the woods, the ones we cleared having been reclaimed by nature but there are plans for even more trails. There are no domestic animals, no cows, goats or horses, and there are no chickens or pheasants. Yet, we had all of these and received tremendous pleasure from them while they were part of the family. We went out of animal and poultry husbandry because we wanted free time to travel without the worry of hiring someone to look after the animals and birds. Happily, the farm is not devoid of feathered friends or animals. Nature, in taking over once cultivated land with her own reforestation design, has added trees, shrubs and canes to attract more birds and animals.

As we sit on the deck marvelling at the changes nature is making, watching a technicolor sunrise across the valley or admiring the gold painted windows of a home on the opposite hill at sunset, we are content. There is much to see — and do.

This is a paradise for writers, artists, thinkers: it is country-quiet, free of the distracting din of city life; an opportunity to stroll acres of fields and woods to refresh the mind and challenge the senses; and the opportunity for sleep and rest beyond belief. Life can be socially active, or very quiet.

Not all dreams can be realized, of course, but if a dream can be turned into a realistic goal, achievement is up to the individual. By any standard, this old farm has given two dreamers the best years of their lives. It wasn't easy! Many sacrifices were necessary, many compromises accepted. These provided a lot of laughs and not a few tears, tempering the steel of our determination to make a dream come true. It also strengthened our love of the land, engraved a deeper appreciation and understanding of nature that have given richer meaning to life itself.

Now there are new and renewed dreams and more time to accomplish them. There are trails to be built, ponds to be rescued, more trees to be planted. The old well must be dug out and reclaimed because we purchased an antique long-handled pump we want to use, a backup water supply. There's time for more sports and plenty of room for a putting green. The horseshoe pitch should be restored. A small greenhouse would add to the pleasure of spring and give us a head start on our gardens.

The Pines is a dream come true — and we're still dreaming!

3 0020 00001 3971